IT'S A HELL OF A MIDLIFE

GOOD TO THE LAST DEATH

BOOK 10

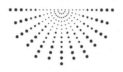

ROBYN PETERMAN

JOIN MY NEWSLETTER FOR THE LATEST RELEASES!

ACKNOWLEDGMENTS

The Good To The Last Death Series is a pleasure to write. It's A Hell of a Midlife was a joy and an obsession for me. Telling stories is my passion and my passion has been fulfilled with this series. Daisy, Gideon and the gang bring me an absurd amount of joy and I hope you feel the same way. See some old friends and meet some new ones!

As always, writing may be a solitary sport, but it takes a whole bunch of people to make the magic happen.

Renee — Thank you for my beautiful cover and for being the best badass critique partner in the world. TMB. LOL

Wanda — You are the freaking bomb. Love you to the moon and back.

Heather, Nancy, Caroline, Susan and Wanda — Thank you for reading early and helping me find the booboos. You all rock.

My Readers — Thank you for loving the stories that come from my warped mind. It thrills me.

Steve, Henry and Audrey — Your love and support makes all of this so much more fun. I love you people endlessly.

DEDICATION

For Steve. You are my real-life hero. Thank you for putting up with my crazy.

MORE IN THE GOOD TO THE LAST DEATH SERIES

BOOK DESCRIPTION

IT'S A HELL OF A MIDLIFE

I did *not* order the extra slice of Armageddon to go with my midlife crisis. Apparently, if you're an Immortal, it comes free of charge.

I have until sundown tomorrow to get to a parallel plane of existence, save my family, and kick bad-guy butt all before the world ends.

Impossible, right?

Not according to my posse of whackado buddies. They like to remind me that nothing is impossible as long as I believe.

Well, I'm about to be the mother of all believers.

Armed with nothing but a folder titled 'Sh*t Pile' and backed by a few fabulous drag queens, a toothpick-chewing nutjob, a sweetheart with a penchant for sharing disgusting facts, and an ice queen who doesn't play nice with others, we have our work cut out for us.

Time is not on my side, and I am having one hell of a midlife crisis.

CHAPTER ONE

THE STORM CREATED ITS OWN EERIE SONG IN THE BRANCHES
of the leafless winter trees. It was a warning to stay inside.
That wasn't an option. If I wanted to see the sun, I had to
weather the storm. The storm wasn't allowed in my home.
Period.

"I'm going outside," I said, quickly pulling on a jacket. "I
want a ward put around the house for protection. Charlie,
Candy, Heather and Tim, can you do that?"

Choosing the Immortal Enforcer, the Keeper of Fate, the
Arbitrator between Heaven and Hell and the Immortal
Courier wasn't random. As the Angel of Mercy, I was a
rookie who hadn't even read the Bible, much to everyone's
shock. It was on my *very* long to-do list. While I might be
powerful, I was only forty. The combined age of my friends
was something I had a difficult time wrapping my mind
around. Right now, power *and* experience were pivotal.

I hoped the ward would protect the house in this plane

and in the one that held the love of my life. Gideon, Gabe, Zadkiel, the unnamed woman who I'd mentally called Cat, and the ghosts needed to stay safe. If the house went down, I wasn't sure that was possible. It also had the potential of keeping the monster from his hoard. If he wasn't able to get to them, he might not be able to destroy them.

"Yes, Daisy, we can," Charlie said, putting on his coat and barking out instructions. "Everyone outside. Candy, go to the back of the house. Tim, right side. Heather, left. I'll stay toward the front but hidden from sight." He checked his watch. "In two minutes from now, cast the spell. We must do it at the same time. Leave about six feet of buffer. When the house is warded, go to the front yard."

"Roger that," Candy said, sprinting out of the back door.

Tim and Heather used the same exit.

"Tory and Dirk, flank me," I said, moving to the front door as Charlie used the kitchen door. Tory was a wild card. She was also known as Purgatory—a tragic job in the Immortal realm. However, she'd been proving her loyalty repeatedly as of late. While I didn't completely trust her, I trusted her enough. Dirk aka Death was one of the Four Horsemen of the Apocalypse. He was not only a fearsome being, but also a fabulous drag queen. I'd trust him with the life of my child. The life of my child was more important than my own.

"Always, darling," Dirk said with his horns on fire.

For a brief moment, I wondered if the rain would extinguish the flame and ruin his dress. It was a random thought and made me chuckle. In the midst of war, the little things that made me think helped me stay calm. I pinched my weenus for extra piece of mind—a bizarre move I'd learned from the drag queens. Who knew that elbow skin couldn't feel pain no matter how hard it was pinched? It wasn't great since I was wearing a coat, but it helped.

"What are you doing?" Tory asked.

"Squeezing my weenus," I replied.

"Brilliant!" Dirk squealed as he pinched his own. "The magic of the weenus cannot be denied!"

Tory rolled her eyes but pinched her weenus. It was absurd. We were some of the most powerful people on the planet, yet, we were gripping our elbow skin like it was a magic bullet. Whatever. It certainly couldn't hurt.

I opened the door and walked into the storm.

"Gideon, I'm doing this for you. I love you."

There was no answer. Under normal circumstances, we could silently communicate. Circumstances were anything but normal. While we were both technically in the same place, he was caught on a different plane being drained of his magic by the monster.

Beyond unacceptable.

I'd hoped for an answer from him but hadn't expected it. My words held true whether he could hear me or not.

The nighttime sky was blacker than usual. The stars had hidden, and the moon wasn't visible. The wind was as furious as a hurricane. It tore through the landscape with a frenzied high-pitched screech. Trees uprooted as the gales screamed a tune that would visit my nightmares. The gorgeous oaks and willows twisted in the violent gusts and shattered into kindling.

I felt a jolt of energy as the ward dropped around the

house. My sigh of relief was momentary when I realized Agnes hadn't stayed inside.

"Agnes," I shouted over the storm. "Go into the light. NOW."

The thought of the ghost being destroyed terrified me. She still had a chance. The blinding yellow glow surrounded her and kept her safe from the vicious weather. However, I didn't think it would keep her safe from the monster. Tory turned and pushed against the ward to find a spot to shove Agnes back in. It was futile. Charlie, Heather, Candy and Tim didn't screw around. It was impenetrable.

"Puddin'," Agnes said far too calmly for what was going down. "I can't. I need to see how the story ends. Need my curiosity satisfied. I'm an author in life and death, sweetie."

There was no time to fight with her.

With the storm overhead, it was difficult to be heard. I glanced wildly around for Tar Basilisk. He'd said he would come, but monsters couldn't be trusted... He wasn't there. Or at least not where I could see him. The crashes of lightning and the booms of the thunder were so loud, I put my hands over my ears. It didn't help. Being in the middle of the raging storm seemed like a stupid plan, but it was also the only plan we had.

Candy, Tim, Charlie and Heather had joined us in the front yard. Everyone scanned the turbulent landscape, searching for the monster.

"Where is the fucker?" Candy bellowed.

No one had an answer.

The rain came down in torrents, soaking us to the skin. I barely felt it. My most fervent wish was that it would wash away the vile situation we were in. That wasn't going to happen. That wasn't the job of the rain. It was my job.

Charlie touched my back and pointed. "The field," he shouted. "I think the field is the eye of the storm."

Cupping my hands above my eyes so I could see through the downpour, I looked in the direction he pointed. He was correct. It appeared that the field where Gideon and Gabe had disappeared was the quiet eye of the deadly storm.

"Follow me," I shouted to my small but powerful army. We stood a better chance without the wind blowing us around like rag dolls.

I was faster than everyone and made it to the field in seconds. Tar Basilisk appeared in an explosion of black and golden glitter. He glanced around in shock and fury. When his gaze landed on me, his eyes narrowed to slits.

I was struck by the unusual colors of his eyes—one glowed gold, one was sparkling blood-red. He was a mix of species, Angel and Demon... just like my daughter. The man's outer beauty was undeniable. However, his pretty exterior belied his putrid insides.

"Was this necessary?" he demanded, waving his hand at the storm raging all around the outer rim of the field.

"I could ask you the same question," I ground out.

He appeared confused. I wasn't buying it. The monster had gotten away with his evil for thousands of years. Playing games was in his nature. I was going to beat him this time.

"Stop the storm," he growled.

I rolled my eyes. "I didn't start it, asshole. That's on you."

Where were the others? I didn't want to take my eyes off

of the dangerous prize, but it was odd they weren't here yet. I took the chance to glance over my shoulder and gasped. They were about forty feet away and unable to reach me. The monster had dropped a bubble around us. I no longer had backup to fight the evil man. I was on my own. The only positive was that the storm was outside of the bubble. I had a better chance of defeating him if I wasn't blinded by the rain. I slid out of my coat. It was soaked and weighed me down.

Tar Basilisk glowed dangerously as a fire of his own making licked up his large body. I'd never seen anything like it. The red and orange flames danced over his jeans and parka but didn't come close to setting him ablaze. His power was evident. It was massive.

So was mine.

The man appeared unhinged. That was fine. I could use it to my advantage. If he lost control, he'd be sloppy and emotional. Being emotional and sloppy equated to being dead. The Goddess Lilith said to separate the head and the heart. It was exactly what I was going to do.

I gauged the bubble around us to be about the size of half a football field. A grove of pine trees was behind the enemy. A slight movement in the tree line caught my eye— and my heart sank.

Micky Muggles had not left the property. I'd known the redneck idiot since high school. The mullet sporting man had just been fired from the police department for having sex in his cruiser with women who were not his wife. I'd stupidly let him spend the night on my property in his car. When I couldn't find his car earlier, I'd thought he'd left. I

was wrong. He'd obviously moved it. I didn't see it
anywhere. He shook like a leaf and had an expression of
terror on his face.

I didn't blame him. This was a lot for an Immortal to
handle. To a human's mind, this had to be a living night-
mare. The only solace I had was that if Micky Muggles
lived, Tim could erase his memories.

Micky waved. I ignored him. Tar wanted the human
dead for some reason. That wasn't going to happen on my
watch. Maybe Micky *had* banged Tar's gal pal. I couldn't
wrap my mind around that, but beauty was in the eye of the
beholder.

I just hoped the idiot had the smarts to stay out of sight.

"Where's your partner in evil?" Tar bellowed.

My fingers sparked, and I could feel a destructive magic
bubbling inside me. It was dark. Abaddon had given me
some of his Demon blood to fight Zadkiel. I was told the
effects would wear off, but I could still feel it entangled with
my own energy. My desire to end the monster warred with
every compassionate tendency I owned. Considering I was
the Angel of Mercy, that was a lot.

I squinted at the Angel/Demon. "I have no evil partner,
asshole."

His roar of fury set the tree line behind him ablaze. Out
of the corner of my eye, I saw a deathly scared Micky
Muggles relocate behind a large rock. I wanted to save the
dummy, but there was too much to lose if I tried. The
bubble around us was unbreakable. All of the Immortals on
the other side were trying to get through, to no avail.

Candy circled the barrier and threw fireballs every

several feet. They bounced right back at her. That didn't stop the Keeper of Fate. Dirk flew above the bubble and tried to tear his way through with his fangs and claws. It was useless. It was also horrifying to glance up and see him in his full badass glory. No movie or book had ever created a being as terrifying as what Dirk had become. The delightful queen was nowhere to be seen. My friend personified Death and then some.

"Give me what's mine, or you will die, you scum," Tar shouted.

"Pot, kettle, black," I shot back.

He didn't like that. Too bad, so sad.

I swallowed back all the other ugly things I wanted to yell. I needed something from him. I needed it badly. To get it, he had to stay alive… for a little while. As much as I wanted to turn him to dust, I needed the ancient spell he had used to create the parallel plane. Without it, I couldn't get to Gideon. Of course, I was working off a piece of fiction that Agnes Bubbala had written. It was all I had, so I was going for it.

Tar thought I had something of his. Maybe I could make a trade… Although, if it was his hoard, then it was a no-go. That didn't make sense, though. If he'd hidden his hoard here, he should be able to get to it. Maybe the ward around the house posed a problem. If so, that was very good news.

"What do I have that's yours?" I asked calmly, holding my sparking hands out in front of me as a warning.

"Playing stupid is beneath you," he snarled. "But I should have expected it. It's shocking that you've been able to hide your true age. How did you do it?"

"What the hell are you talking about?" I hissed.

"You're not forty. More like forty thousand," he said icily. "How did you fool the Grim Reaper? Is Gideon a complete imbecile?"

This dude wasn't working on all cylinders. He was nuts. I looked damned good for forty. My brain raced with all the ways I could handle the bizarre situation. Gram had said that lying wasn't smart and that the truth was easier to remember, but that was when one was dealing with a sane individual. Tar Basilisk wasn't sane. He was the opposite.

I decided to play along. Although, I stayed just vague enough not to enrage him. He was already a loose cannon. "Age is just a number. Unimportant."

I hadn't even lied. Gram would approve.

He laughed. It was ugly.

I rolled my eyes. I shouldn't have.

In the millisecond that I took my eyes off the man, he sent a zap of magic in my direction that threw me against the side of the bubble like a ball out of a cannon. I was sure a few of my ribs were broken. Getting air into my lungs was a chore. However, two could play his game.

I jumped to my feet and ignored the searing pain in my torso. I wiggled my fingers. A massive tree came down on the monster with a sickening thud and trapped him beneath it. I wasn't a fool. He wouldn't be down for long. Slashing my hands through the air, I sent a bolt of electricity that exploded when it hit him.

He slammed the ground with his fists and caused a massive crater beneath my feet. As I fell in, I threw another electrocution his way. He roared his displeasure and dove into the crater.

This wasn't going to end well. He advanced on me like a rabid animal. Snapping my fingers, I levitated out of the hole. The monster was right behind me.

My fury bubbled up to the surface. The hideous man was trying his best to end me. He'd taken Gideon and Gabe. He'd destroyed so many over the centuries. I wasn't going to be part of the Collector's collection.

I froze for a moment. A strange déjà vu came over me, but I couldn't pinpoint what it was. The keyword was collection. However, a fireball the size of an SUV was headed my way and needed to be avoided. Figuring out a déjà vu wasn't on the agenda. Staying alive was.

We were both bleeding profusely. The banging and shouting on the other side of the bubble was loud. Understanding it was impossible. It was garbled. I couldn't spare a glance. Looking away from the monster would be the last thing I did. I was sure of it.

Blow after blow was traded. We both gave as good as we got. I pictured Gideon and our daughter, Alana Catherine in my mind. They were who I fought for. The monster couldn't win.

My exhaustion was real. My body felt sluggish. Tar Basilisk was as strong as I was, if not stronger. Out of the corner of my eye, I saw Agnes Bubbala losing her shit. She was screaming and crying. She should have stayed in the house. This was too much for a human mind to take in— even a dead one.

The shot of magic Tar sent hit me in the stomach. I

leaned forward and threw up.

He laughed.

I was done.

Slashing both hands through the air, I envisioned razor-sharp blades of fire. As if on command, they appeared in my waiting hands. With a scream of fury and fatigue, I threw them, aiming for his arms. They sliced right through and lopped the appendages off. The shocked expression on his bloody and bruised face would have been funny if the situation wasn't so deadly serious. I conjured up two more of the fiery weapons and removed the monster's legs.

Tar Basilisk was now a stump with a head.

He was pissed.

The appendages would grow back. He was Immortal.

Right now, it was information time.

Limping over to the bastard, I stopped a few feet away. I wasn't taking any chances.

"Give me the spell," I said flatly.

He writhed on the ground in pain. It was hard to watch, and I didn't like knowing I was responsible. However, it was me or him, and I preferred me.

"I'll trade myself for her," he begged. "I'm far more powerful. It's me you want."

Was he delirious? What was he talking about?

"Who?" I asked, wildly confused.

He glared at me. Even without arms and legs, he was terrifying. I took a cautious step back.

"Catriona," he snapped. "Trade me for my sister. You don't need her in your hoard if you have me."

It felt as if I was having an out-of-body experience.

Gideon had said the woman had uttered the word cat. Was she trying to say Catriona? Was this man not the monster? Was he trying to do the same thing I was doing? Had I royally fucked up, as Candy Vargo would say? I moved quickly to Tar Basilisk and squatted down next to him.

"You're the Collector," I whispered.

He shook his head. "*You* are the Collector."

"I'm not," I said, unsure whether to trust him. "On my life, I'm not." My gut said he was also telling the truth, but my gut had been on the iffy side lately. "Your name—Tar Basilisk—it means dragon. A dragon collects hoards."

"My name is Zander," he said. "I used the name to draw the monster out. I felt its presence here."

"The hoard is here," I confirmed. "On a parallel plane in my home. My mate and my brother are in it. I'm trying to get them out."

We stared at each other in silence, trying to figure out if the other was lying.

"Break the bubble," I told him.

"I didn't create it," he said.

I inhaled deeply. If he hadn't—which I wasn't sure I believed—who had? Who was screwing with us? Or was I being naïve? The Collector was an excellent actor and liar.

I backed away from the man who called himself Zander and kept my eyes on him. He couldn't throw magic since he had no arms, but trusting him completely could easily be my final mistake.

When I got to the side of the bubble and took a quick look, the light around Agnes Bubbala grew almost blinding. All of my friends and family pointed and gestured frantically at her. She was talking a mile a minute, and I wasn't a terrific lip reader. I used my hands to indicate that she needed to slow down.

She did. And what she had to say changed everything.

"Mr. Handyman," she mouthed, pointing to the far side of the bubble.

My head whipped around, and my eyes landed on Micky Muggles. He stepped out from behind the rock and waved. My stomach lurched, and I shuddered with disgust.

I'd sworn I wouldn't be stupid, but I had been. I'd been very stupid. All of the clues... the words I should have collected had been right under my nose in plain sight. The illusion had tricked me. And I'd dismembered the one Immortal who the Collector feared.

Micky Muggles smiled. It was oily and triumphant.

All the words I should've collected but missed came roaring to the forefront of my brain. The déjà vu hit me like a ton of bricks. Collections were the key. He was a collector. He'd told me himself.

Micky Muggles had laid it all out. *Nickname, the Draaagoon.* The sadistic man had told me he was the dragon. *Thank you, Daisy. Thank you so much. The Draaagoon, thanks you!*

I'm a collector, he had said. *Beer cans, rabbits' feet and beautiful chest-blessed women, among other things. Can't call me stupid even though my ex-wife does.* The "other things" were what I should have paid attention to.

Agnes' words held more weight now as well... *Love can blind people. Today, I'd describe him as short, stinky and stuck in a time warp. I mean, some might say I'm a fashion faux pas with my big hair and all, but Mr. Handyman takes the cake.* The time warp was the 1980s. Micky Muggles' mullet was as bad as Agnes' teased and sprayed hairdo.

Tim's words were prophetic. I just didn't know at the time. *The name, the aggressive behavior, the fact that he's Immortal... all important. If Tar Basilisk is not the monster—I feel like he could lead us to him.*

The words I'd missed danced in my head and mocked me. My lack of awareness could end those I loved the most. On top of that, I'd hurt someone badly who wasn't the monster. Granted, he'd hurt me, too, thinking I was the monster. It was so incredibly senseless it was hard to absorb.

My stomach roiled, and my body shook with rage. Without Zander, I wouldn't have found the Collector.

According to Agnes, the reason her fictional character Parveit, Lord of The Red was able to get away with being such a shit for so long was that he was able to hide his essence. He hid in plain sight. He was able to disguise who he was. He got others to trust him. That's when he struck. He was able to slide under the radar for many moons. The Handyman aka Mickey Muggles had helped her write that book. He'd told his own story under the guise of fiction.

Micky Muggles had slid under the radar for far more than many moons.

"Well, now," Micky Muggles said, walking across with field with a pep in his step and an evil glint in his eyes. "Have you figured it out, Angel of Mercy?"

My title on his lips made me want to hurl.

"You're the Collector," I stated flatly.

"Bingo," he replied gleefully, pulling a quarter out from behind his ear and offering it to me.

When I didn't take it, he dropped it on the ground and sneered. "Thought you had better manners than that, Daisy. You sure did back in high school."

"You thought wrong," I ground out, wondering if I could take him.

He grinned. "I've been waitin' on you to come into your power for a long time. It's simply delicious." He licked his lips and winked.

He still seemed human to me—repulsive and human. I detected no Immortal footprint and couldn't gauge his power. The word illusion had come up with both Lilith and the Oracle. Its importance wasn't lost on me. The Collector was a master of illusion. He'd hidden who he was, and he'd somehow hidden his footprint.

The imbecile I'd known since high school stared at me. It occurred to me the Collector might not have any power at all. It could be why he continually stole it from others. However, he'd created the storm and the bubble. Was that his power or had he used up what he'd stolen from Catriona, Gideon and Gabe?

I wished I knew.

If wishes were horses, beggars would ride.

If I wanted something to happen, I had to make it happen. Micky was a talker. I'd get him to talk and pray that his arrogance would reveal what I needed.

"Why did you kill Agnes Bubbala?" I asked.

The Collector/ Mr. Handyman shrugged and waved at Agnes. She spat on the ground from outside the bubble and flipped him off. "She killed me in her book. I returned the favor."

"From where I'm standing, you're unfortunately alive."

He chuckled. It was a hollow and obsequious sound. "I'm Parveit, Lord of the Red."

I couldn't help it. I rolled my eyes. "He's a fictional character."

"Was he?" the Collector inquired with an arched brow. "I think not. Agnes should never have killed him. I told her over and over it was wrong. She said the bad guys have to lose, and the good guys have to win. The bitch also said that love conquers all. She was incorrect. And now she's dead. Funny how the good guys tend to lose in real life..."

"Hilarious," I snapped. It was difficult to take an asshole with a combover seriously. However, I had to. He'd somehow abducted the Grim Reaper and the Archangel.

Over Micky's shoulder, I could see that Zander was healing. I needed him to mend faster. Maybe if I kept the idiot Collector monologuing, Zander could become whole enough to fight the monster with me. After all, our goal was the same.

"How do you do it?" I asked, trying my damnedest to feign real interest.

The Collector cupped his crotch and leered at me. "Read the book. It's all in there. Every single bit."

Hubris mixed with stupidity was a scary combo. I was still unsure if he was truly simple-minded or if it was an act. I was going with an act. There was no way he was as brainless as he presented himself.

"Seriously," I said, ignoring his comment. It was a risk,

but I was going for the dumb-girly angle. He'd bought it at the scene of the crime when the queens had stolen the horses, and he might buy it now. I already felt dirty, and I hadn't even started. Flirting with people who sported mullets and killed Immortals and humans wasn't my forte, but tonight it was going to be. The Collector's ego was enormous.

My goal was to be a better actor than him. "It's just brilliant. I don't know another Immortal who can do what you do. I'm in awe."

The scrawny jerk puffed out his chest. "It's nothing," he replied in an "aw shucks" tone.

I swallowed my bile and kept going. Zander had regenerated one leg and part of an arm. I didn't know how much longer I could keep Micky talking, but I was going to try to make it long enough for Zander to grow back his appendages. Backup would be welcome right now.

"No," I said with a giggle. "It's not nothing. Tell me! I'm so impressed."

The Collector morphed from Micky Muggles into me. There was no fanfare. No sparks, just a quick blink of his eyes. I was looking at an exact replica of myself. It was surreal. He then morphed into Zander. From Zander, he became Tory. And he finished it off as Agnes.

"Easy as pie," he crowed as he morphed back into Micky Muggles.

"Wow!" I squealed, clapping my hands, much to his delight. "Is Micky Muggles the real you?"

The Collector grew perturbed and angry. Shit, what had I said that pissed him off?

"What's wrong with Micky Muggles?" he shouted.

I held up my hands. "Nothing. Nothing is wrong with Micky Muggles. Micky's a great guy—very handsome."

The lie stuck in my mouth like sandpaper. A gaslit Collector was better than a furious one. Flipping my hair like I'd seen the queens do multiple times, I giggled again. "Was that you at my old farmhouse? Were you checking out my old digs, you dirty old man?"

Micky recovered quickly from his tantrum and flexed his muscles. "Yep! I was gonna take your dead grandma hostage for collateral. But them ghosts just up and disappeared."

It took all I had not to dive at the bastard and rip his head off with my bare hands. Separate the heart and the head, I reminded myself. "Ingenious," I said with a little shimmy that made me feel like an ass, but the Collector bought it hook, line and sinker.

"I thought so, too," he said with a pleased nod. "Didn't know you'd be so amiable, Daisy… and so hot to trot."

I shrugged and batted my eyes. "I guess you don't know me."

"Sure would like to," he replied, grabbing his crotch again.

I was going to need to shower for a week if I came out of this alive. "I want my own hoard, Micky. Tell me how to make my own hoard."

"It's easy," he said with a boastful grin. "But you're gonna have to get naked for that info."

I threw up a little in my mouth. "Too cold out here," I said quickly.

"My car is parked over there," he said, pointing beyond the still-smoldering pines. "We could get in a quickie before I need to skedaddle."

This was headed in a seriously bad direction. "Tell me the spell, and I'll take off my shirt."

"I sure do like 'em horny," he said. "But I'm gonna need more than a titty shot to share my secrets."

If I agreed to go to his car, he'd have to disintegrate the bubble. I'd have my army back. Was he thinking with his dick or his brain? It certainly appeared that his little head was in control of his big head. I was about to find out. Zander was finally fully regenerated and standing about twenty feet away.

Maybe the army wasn't needed. Candy Vargo would eat Micky Muggles without thinking. She was literally spewing fire. I had no intention of banging the Collector, but I needed the spell. If I had to do a strip tease and remove a single piece of clothing for each word of the spell, I'd do it, and then end him. I was mad at myself for removing my coat. Quickly picking it back up, I put the soggy down-filled mess back on.

Wait...

Words. Collect the words. I hadn't done it right yet, but there was no time to start like the present. The Collector had just said I needed to read the book... it was all in there. It was a risk, but he was so damned conceited, he'd most likely given it all away to Agnes. It was perilous to believe that the actual spell was in the book, but if he'd used the term enchanted thaumaturgy bands, there was better than a 50/50 chance that he'd revealed all.

"Full disclosure," Micky said, unzipping his pants and adjusting his erection. "I ain't gonna show you my hoard. That one is pretty much dead. In fact, if it ain't dead now, it will be by sundown tomorrow."

Not often in my life had I seen red, but Micky's words undid me.

I'd bank on the book. It was time for the Collector to die. Violently.

Fortunately, Zander had the same plan. His roar of fury shook the bubble and caused a five-alarm fire to explode to life. Before I could even move, Zander had the Collector by the throat and was ready to rip it out.

"I will kill you like you killed my sister," he snarled, shaking Micky as if he weighed only a pound.

Zander snapped Micky's legs and arms. The disgusting little man screamed in agony. Zander was just getting started.

"I will make you suffer before I end you," he shouted as he head-butted the broken man.

Micky flew across the field like a paper doll in the wind. His terrified shrieks were unsettling. I couldn't find it in me to care. He was never going to share the spell. It didn't matter if he was dead. The spell was in the book. He'd said it himself.

Zander ran at him so fast that he disappeared from sight for a second. His fists connecting to Micky Muggles' face were sickening.

"No," Zander shouted in horror. "Oh my God, no!"

I ran as fast as he had. I stopped short and screamed. On the ground was a beautiful woman. She looked almost identical to Zander. Her legs and arms were broken. Her face was bloodied from being punched. She was moaning and crying. She held her hands in front of her face and begged for her life.

"Zander," she gasped out, coughing up blood. "It's me, Catriona. Please stop. Please. Don't kill me."

Zander tried to crawl to his sister. I stepped in front of him and blocked him. "Separate the head from the heart or both will break," I said harshly. "It's not her."

"How do you know?" he demanded with tears running down his handsome face. "Tell me you're sure. Tell me you would bet your daughter's life that she is not my sister. Tell me," he bellowed.

I couldn't. I wouldn't bet my daughter's life on anything. And the truth was that I wasn't sure. Had the Collector screwed with us and tricked Zander into beating his sister to within an inch of her life? Or had he simply morphed into Catriona?

"I don't think it's her," I finally said in a whisper.

"Help me, Zander," she begged. "Please, help me."

Zander shoved me aside. I hit the wet ground like a sack of potatoes. "*Think* is not good enough, Angel of Mercy," he hissed at me.

My heart felt like it was lodged in my throat as I watched Zander gently pick up his sister and cradle her close. If it was Gideon on the ground, I wasn't sure if I'd have the strength to stay back, but the word illusion had been beaten into my brain by multiple powerful entities.

Catriona sobbed in her brother's arms. It seemed so real... until it didn't.

In the blink of an eye, the woman in Zander's arms disappeared, and the Collector was in her place. Zander was so filled with self-hatred and remorse he hadn't noticed that he was lovingly rocking Micky Muggles in his arms.

"Zander," I screamed.

His head jerked to the left, and he glared at me with fury. He still didn't know.

It wasn't until the Collector laughed that he realized his fatal mistake. Micky chanted a spell, and they disappeared in a flash of green mist. In the wind after they were out of sight, I heard Micky whisper, "See ya. Wouldn't wanna be ya. You're next, Daisy."

I dropped to my knees as the bubble disintegrated. Dirk and Candy Vargo were the first to get to me.

"Motherfucker!" Candy shouted. She waved her hands and put out the fire.

Dirk carefully helped me to my feet and hugged me close. He was still in his terrifying form, but his arms around me made me feel safe and loved. "I've got you, darling."

"Agnes," I muttered against his chest. "Is Agnes still here?"

"Barely," Heather said as she looked me over for wounds. "Tim," she called out. "We need some healing over here, please."

"Not now." I extracted myself from Dirk's embrace and glanced around wildly. I spotted the golden glow immediately. It was fading fast and taking Agnes with it. "Don't go, Agnes," I yelled. "I need you."

Grabbing a still-cussing Candy Vargo by the neck of her

26

sweatshirt, I dragged her over to where Agnes was growing fainter by the second. Candy had read the books. All of them. "Was there a spell in *Dragons Do it Drunk?*" I asked her.

"What are you talkin' about, jackass?" Candy asked.

My head felt like it was going to explode. Nothing was going right. I had one more chance, and that chance was about to vanish.

"Agnes, did Mr. Handyman ever share the spell with you? The ancient one he used to create the parallel planes?"

"Spell. Yes!" she said.

Her voice sounded so far away. She kept talking, but I couldn't make out the words. The light was wrapping her in its warm embrace. For the first time since I'd become the Death Counselor, I despised the golden light. It was about to take away the information I needed to save Gideon.

"Yes," I said as tears of frustration and fear ran down my cheeks. It felt like I was having a panic attack combined with a nervous breakdown. My legs no longer wanted to hold me up. I held onto Candy Vargo, so I wouldn't fall. "Do you know the spell? Can you tell me the spell?"

Agnes' lips were moving. I tried to read them since the sound was muffled, but like before, she was talking too fast. As the glorious light closed in around her in her final moments, I heard three words as clear as day.

"PILE OF SHIT," Agnes bellowed.

And then she disappeared.

I let go of Candy and hit the ground hard. I had no one to blame but myself. Lilith had given me guidance, and I hadn't recognized it when it was under my nose. My gut had told me that it wasn't Catriona on the ground, but I didn't trust it. Now Zander was part of the hoard. I could've stopped it. I hadn't. If the Collector had been telling the truth, then Gideon, Gabe and Zadkiel only had until sundown tomorrow.

"We're fucked," I said, glad that Gram was inside. She might let Candy get away with the F-bomb here and there, but she wasn't fond of me dropping the foul word.

Tim seated himself next to me on the ground and pulled out his notebook. "I beg to differ, friend."

I wasn't following. "Okay, I'll bite and beg you to differ."

Charlie, Heather, Tory, Rafe, Candy and Dirk formed a circle around us.

"Nothing is impossible," Tim reminded me as he took my hand in his. "You just have to believe."

I nodded. I couldn't speak. If I did, I would cry. Right now, separating the head and the heart wasn't working. My heart was breaking, and I was sure my mind would follow. I didn't know what to believe anymore. I knew I needed to stay strong for Alana Catherine, but without Gideon, I felt like half of me was missing. I yearned for his laugh.

"Candy Vargo," Tim said, looking up at her. "Are you positive that the words of the spell are not contained within the pages of the novel, *Dragons Do It Drunk?*"

"Positive," she said. "I've read it about fifty times. No fuckin' spell. I mean, the spell is cast, but the actual spell ain't in there."

If asking Candy was why Tim had begged to differ, I was sticking with my profane prediction of us being fucked.

"The words," Tim said. "It's all in the words."

He stared at me for a long beat and waited. I loved him, but if he was about to dole out something cryptic, I was going to punch him.

He didn't speak. He simply waited.

It hit me as hard as I'd hit the bubble wall when Zander had blasted me. The words… Agnes' words. My body had been through the ringer. I was covered in dried blood, and my ribs were definitely broken, along with a few other bones.

I'd felt better than I had since Gideon's disappearance. There was nothing quite as euphoric as hope renewed.

"Pile of shit," I said with a grin.

Tim's expression matched mine. "Keep going, friend."

"The spell is in the deleted scenes in the Shit Pile folder in Agnes' desk."

"Oh my!" Dirk screamed. "So exciting! Better than an orgasm!"

I stood up and brushed the mud off my pants. There was nothing I could do about the blood. I needed a shower, but that would have to wait.

"Who's coming with me?" I asked.

"Where you goin', jackass?" Candy Vargo asked, handing me a toothpick.

The question was redundant. The Keeper of Fate knew exactly where I was going.

I put the toothpick into my mouth and flipped her off. "Ohio. Agnes' house. You in?"

"Hell to the fuckin' yes, I'm in," Candy bellowed, handing out toothpicks to everyone.

"I'm in," Tory said with a stick of wood hanging out of her mouth.

It was all wrong but oh so right.

Charlie took over. "Heather, Rafe, Dirk, Prue, Abby and I will stay here and protect the house. I'd suggest Tim goes to Ohio with you, along with Candy and Tory."

I nodded at the Enforcer and hugged him. "Nothing is impossible. I just have to believe."

Charlie hugged me back. "You're correct, Daisy. You must believe in the outcome you want and, more importantly, believe in yourself."

His words were wise. Over the past few days, I'd been running for my midlife. I'd keep running until Gideon, Gabe, Zander, Catriona and even my mortal enemy, Zadkiel, were back safe and sound. That was the outcome I wanted, and I'd accept nothing less.

I looked up at the sky. The storm had subsided, but the stars were still hidden by the clouds. I'd weathered one storm, but there were more on the horizon. I'd take the rain, the wind, the lightning and the thunder gladly. I believed that I would indeed see the full glory of the sun.

Tory, Tim, Candy and I joined hands. The power between us was intense. It was as glorious as the sun. Nothing worthwhile was easy. If it was easy, it wouldn't be worth it. I'd go to the end of the world and back for Gideon. As for now, I was going to Ohio.

"Shit pile, here we come."

CHAPTER TWO

CANDY, IN A SOMEWHAT POLITE MANNER FOR HER, STARTED off the post-transport conversation. "I'd like to point out that we're in a fuckin' car."

"Quite true," Tim agreed.

"I'm gonna bet my left tit, which is the bigger and bouncier one, that Agnes Bubbala didn't live in her fuckin' car," Candy added.

"Everyone, get low. Now," I ordered. There were two police cruisers parked behind us and people inside the house.

Tory, Tim, Candy and I ducked down in the vehicle. Tim and I were in the front. Tory and Candy were in the back.

"Time?" I questioned. It was still dark outside, but I had no clue what hour of the day it was. I knew we were in Ohio and in the same time zone as Georgia, but that was about all I knew.

Tim checked his watch. "Six-thirty AM."

Moving slowly, I peeked out of the driver's side window facing Agnes' house. The lights were on, and I saw uniformed cops milling around through the bay window. The homes on the street weren't all that close to each other. Each sat on a property of approximately two acres. Agnes' yard was filled with trees and rose bushes. The branches were naked and bare in the frigid winter. Come spring, the yard would be lovely. Sadly, she wouldn't see it.

However, we had a bigger problem it seemed. When Tim and I had transported to check on Agnes' home yesterday to look for clues of her demise, we'd found her dead body slumped over her desk. Tim had disguised his voice and called in for a wellness check since she lived alone, and he hadn't heard from her. He'd used a burner phone and posed as her book editor... because he was brilliant.

What wasn't brilliant was that it appeared the police were searching the house when we needed to get in there.

"Cops work at six-thirty in the morning?" I asked, squinting and trying to figure out how many officers were in the house.

"On call all the time," Tim said, closing his eyes and concentrating. "I detect four human heartbeats in the abode."

"Should we kill 'em?" Candy inquired as if that was a normal and sane thing to suggest.

Candy Vargo wasn't normal or sane. I was relieved the Keeper of Fate hadn't suggested eating them.

"Umm... no," I said, running my hand through my wild dark curls. "We're here to get the Shit Pile folder from Agnes' desk, not to end the lives of cops."

"Right. My bad," Candy said. "Guess we're gonna just wait 'em out?"

"Not prudent," Tim said, shaking his head. "We only have until sundown, and the spell we find might be complicated."

I bit down on my bottom lip so I didn't scream. Getting busted by the Ohio men in blue wasn't on the agenda. If we got arrested for trespassing, we'd automatically be suspects in Agnes' death. I knew who'd killed my friend, and I had a plan to avenge her. Micky Muggles would be going down for Agnes' murder and a whole lot of other heinous crimes.

Mess with me... there was a chance I'd forgive. Mess with Gideon and my brother... no such luck.

"Define complicated," I whispered.

Tim shrugged. "I won't know until I see it, friend."

Not the answer I wanted to hear, but Tim never sugar-coated. I loved that about him, but not at the moment. We didn't have time for more complications.

"Spells ain't hard," Candy said, gnawing on a toothpick. "I can do a fuckin' spell naked and twisted up like a pretzel."

I sighed. The visual wasn't pleasant. "Let's hope it doesn't come to that."

Silently, we all tried to come up with a plan. Short of barging in, grabbing the Shit Pile folder and then wiping their minds, I couldn't think of anything. It was an iffy idea with the potential to go sideways fast. The fact they were probably armed was a deterring factor. None of us could die from a gunshot wound and that would be even more suspect than breaking in.

"Quite the conundrum," Tim commented.

If no one had a better idea, we'd have to go with my crappy plan. "Can a mind wipe happen quickly?"

He nodded. "Yes, but I'm concerned someone will immediately call for backup if we enter the house. Six-thirty in the morning is a little odd for a social call."

"Who trusts me?" Tory whispered.

Without missing a beat, Candy, Tim and I all said, "I do."

Tory's expression was one of surprise and shock. Honestly, I was a little shocked at how quickly I'd answered, but realized I meant it.

"Why are you asking?" I demanded. Tory was what I would call an unenthusiastic team player. She did as she was told and not much more. However, she had some skin in this game. She and my brother had been in love a thousand years ago before the former Angel of Mercy, Zadkiel, had tried to destroy them.

He hadn't ended them but had created a devastating distrust that seemed to have broken them beyond repair. I knew Gabe still loved her, but Tory was emotionless on the subject. There was that, along with the fact she wanted Zadkiel to spend the rest of eternity in Purgatory with the Souls of the Martyrs that he'd damned to the tragic and pain-filled destination.

"I can turn myself and one more invisible," she said hesitantly. "The two of us could slip in and get the folder if they can't see us."

"I think it should be Daisy," Tim said.

My lips compressed, and I nodded curtly. "I agree."

"Where's the folder?" Candy Vargo inquired.

"In the room that they're searching. In the desk," I

supplied tightly. "Can we slip through walls and doors if we're invisible?"

Tory nodded. "We can. We can also reach into the drawer without opening it."

"Next fuckin' question," Candy chimed in. "Do we know which drawer of the desk the Shit Pile is in?"

"We don't," Tim said. "But there are only four drawers."

I groaned. "Not really going to help. We need to search through all the paperwork in the drawers to find the right folder. That'll take time. Plus, it might be kind of weird for office supplies to magically float through the room and leave the house."

Candy scratched her nose with the toothpick she'd just removed from her mouth. "Well now, I'm thinkin' Tim and I could cause a ruckus out in the street. Get them coppers out of the house."

I winced. Candy Vargo's idea of a ruckus usually ended in bloodshed and missing limbs. Long before I'd been born, she'd run Tim over with a chariot and lopped off both of his legs. They laughed about it now. I didn't. "Does the ruckus include dismemberment?"

I had to ask.

Candy and Tim both chuckled. Immortals were nuts. "Hell to the no," she promised. "We can just act like a drunk married couple beatin' the crap out of each other. You know, I can wallop Tim because he cheated on me or some shit like that."

"Not the most plausible thing I've heard," I said.

Candy Vargo raised a brow. "You got something better, asscrack?"

I shook my head.

"I do," Tim said. "We could be out for a morning jog, and Candy falls and breaks her leg. I shall then notice the police cars and run up to the house for assistance."

Candy pointed at him with her toothpick. "I like it. Makes more sense, and it's far less bloody." She snapped her fingers. She and Tim were now sporting matching sweatsuits and running shoes. Unfortunately, she'd also given each of them bright green headbands. "I'll scream like I'm fuckin' dyin'."

"Do you think all four cops will go out into the street?" Tory asked, concerned. "If one or two stay back, we're still in a bad position."

Candy Vargo grinned and flicked her nasty toothpick at Tory. "You ain't see me do my thing, girlie. You got nothing to worry about. Just haul your invisible asses into Agnes' house and find that Shit Pile folder fast."

I nodded and pushed away all the horrible thoughts of everything that could go wrong five minutes from now. The clock was ticking. Hell, I was so desperate for the spell, I was close to telling Candy she could eat them. Close... but not quite there.

I glanced over at Tory. "Is going invisible painful?" I was going to do it no matter what. However, it would be nice to know if it was agonizing.

"No pain. No gain," she replied flatly.

"Figures," I muttered. Leaning over to Candy, I removed the new toothpick that she'd shoved into her mouth. I didn't need her choking on top of maiming herself. She flipped me off and grinned. "Are you really going to break your leg?"

"Oh yes," Tim said, rubbing his hands together with glee. "A little bit of payback is in order this fine morning."

Candy Vargo rolled her eyes. "If I let you crack my femur, are you gonna quit your bitchin' about the dang chariot accident, boy?"

"Hardly an *accident*," Tim replied with a chuckle. "But yes, I shall refrain from reminding you that you sliced off both of my legs with a chariot."

Tory wrinkled her nose. "You two are best friends?"

"Absofuckinglutely," Candy said, slapping Tim on the back. "Till the end."

Tim smiled at his deranged buddy. "In exactly five minutes, Candy and I shall start the street show. Is that enough time for you, Tory?"

She nodded. My stomach felt wonky at the impending pain, but it was a tiny price to pay to get the spell to save Gideon. Pain I could take. Losing Gideon... I could not.

"Can either of you whistle?" Tim asked.

I held up my hand. "I can."

"Excellent," he replied. "Once the folder is in hand, whistle. We'll transport back."

Sucking my bottom lip into my mouth, I touched Tim's shoulder. "Umm... don't we need to wipe their minds?"

He giggled. "I'll take care of that. Not to worry."

"Let's get this fuckin' party started," Candy Vargo grunted, cracking her knuckles. "I need my jackass buddy to snap my leg."

Tim waved his hand. He and Candy disappeared from the car.

"With friends like that, who needs enemies?" Tory said, taking my hands in hers.

I laughed. She'd made a decent point, but she didn't know Candy Vargo and Tim as well as I did. They were a perfect BFF match—crazy to the core and as loyal as they came.

She squeezed my hands as her gaze bored into mine. Her piercing blue eyes seemed to spit sparkling diamonds. Her beauty was otherworldly. Tory had an unusual way of fading into the background, but when you truly looked at her, she was stunning. An icy breeze whipped through the car. The windows weren't open. It was magic and it was freaking freezing. I'd secretly named her the Ice Queen upon our first encounter. She was living up to the moniker right down to her shiny silver hair.

"Close your eyes, Daisy," she whispered. "When I tell you to open them, we'll be invisible to the naked eye."

"Will I be able to see you?" I asked, worried. There were about a thousand ways this could go wrong and losing each other was only one of them.

"You will, but I won't look like I do right now."

"Okay... can you be a little less cryptic?" It drove me nuts the way the Immortals conversed. I was a get-to-the-point kind of gal. They tended to go the mysterious, hard to understand and ridiculously confusing route. I was over that crap.

The corners of her lips turned up. The woman rarely smiled. "I'll look like an outline of myself, but it will glow silver."

"Got it. What will I look like?"

Tory shrugged. "Not sure."

Her answer made sense, but I had a few more questions. "You said we can walk through closed doors and walls."

"Correct," she replied.

"Can we physically open the drawers? It would go a heck of a lot faster if we could open them and search for the folder."

"Yes," she confirmed. "You can do anything that you can normally do in your physical body... and a whole lot more."

"Last question," I said, checking the time on my phone. "How long will it last?"

"Until I reverse it."

I eyed her for a long moment. She stared right back.

"And you *will* reverse it," I said with a raised brow.

Her slight smile turned into a laugh. "I *will* reverse it. You have my word."

I squeezed her hands. "Let's do it."

PAIN WAS THE UNDERSTATEMENT OF THE CENTURY. GOING into the Darkness with the ghosts when I entered their minds was agonizing. Becoming invisible was as close to unbearable as I'd ever travelled.

However, I didn't make a sound. Tory had chanted a few melodic words I didn't understand and then it felt like knives dipped in acid and fire shredded me from the inside out. I was certain I'd been seared to a pile of ash. I hadn't. While it seemed to go on forever, I knew it didn't—maybe a few seconds at the most. Worst few seconds I'd experienced.

The method might have been heinous, but the results were perfect. I was an outline of my human body in shimmering gold.

It was fast. It was violent. It worked.

"Holy shit," I choked out, trying hard to catch my breath. "You weren't kidding about the pain."

"I don't kid," Tory replied. She squeezed my hands again. "The gold is lovely. Are you okay?"

I laughed. It was weak, but I still had it. "Define okay."

If anyone had told me a year ago that I'd be invisible inside of a dead woman's car while waiting for Tim to snap Candy Vargo's leg so I could steal a folder labeled Shit Pile, I would have called the looney bin and had that person committed.

That was last year.

This was today.

"Can you move your arms and legs?" Tory asked.

I tried them out. "Yep. I can move and I feel pretty good."

"Now we wait," she said as she took my hand and we floated out of the car without opening the door.

It was the strangest sensation. I felt like the ghosts who came to me for help. It was bizarre and kind of wonderful. We watched Candy Vargo and Tim as we got close to the house without going in. The minute it was clear of cops we would go to work.

Tory gripped my hand tight as we watched in horrified silence. Candy got on her knees in the middle of the road then extended her right leg out in front of her. It looked like she was going to stretch. She wasn't. Tim stood about twenty feet away and did a few jumping jacks to warm up.

Part of me didn't want to watch. However, the other part of me couldn't turn away.

Neither the Keeper of Fate nor the Courier between the Darkness and the Light made a noise. It felt like we were watching a silent B horror flick. Tim squatted low and took the position a runner would at the start of a race. His expression was serious and focused. Candy Vargo's demeanor was calm, cool and collected. Not a huge surprise. She was batshit crazy. I'd be sweating bullets if I knew I was about to get my femur cracked.

"I'm not sure I can watch this," Tory muttered.

"I'm not sure I can't," I replied with a shudder. I'd literally been in wars with Demons and Angels. The fact that I was squeamish about watching my friends maim each other for a greater good was strange. I knew Candy Vargo would heal quickly, but it was still stomach-churning.

As absurd as the scene was it was also a testament to how much we all cared for each other. The way we showed our love and loyalty was way out of the ordinary and seriously disturbing, but no less beautiful. Candy was letting Tim break her leg for Gideon, Gabe, Agnes and the rest of us. It took an army of crazy to keep the world in balance.

I was proud to be part of it. Midlife was a journey—and the crisis was definitely included.

"This is about to get bad," Tory whispered.

It was but it got even weirder first. With a snap of her fingers, Candy Vargo went from a slim and trim looking gal to a very large woman—easily over three hundred pounds. Tim gave her a thumbs up and she gave him the finger. I didn't know what their game plan was, but that didn't impact my role in the overall scheme. They were drawing the cops out of the house and we were getting the folder.

Tim counted down from three with his fingers and began to run. I held my breath. It was sickening to watch my mild-mannered friend jump high into the air and land with both feet and all of his weight on Candy's knee. The crunching sound was positively gruesome. The fact that her knee now bent the wrong way made me throw up in my mouth a little bit. Tory's grip got tighter and I heard her gag.

However, our reactions were nothing compared to the Keeper of Fate's. Her scream followed by a string of swear words that would make a sailor pass out was so loud I jumped and almost fell off the front porch.

All four cops ran out of the front door with their guns drawn.

"Oh my God!" Tim shrieked. "My wife... I think my wife broke her leg. We were jogging and she fell. HELP US!"

Candy's screams of agony were real. Tim's tears and hysteria were also real.

"Jesus," one of the cops muttered. "Look at that knee."

"Call an ambulance," another ordered.

All four holstered their guns and jogged over to where Candy was writhing on the ground.

"I need to get up," she screamed, as two of the cops turned to go back into the house. "The road is dirty. I can't be on a dirty road."

"HELP HER," Tim wailed. "My wife has OCD. She can't be on the dirty road. SHE JUST CAN'T."

"Umm... sir," one of the cops said. "I don't think we should move your wife until the ambulance gets here."

"Not sure we *can* move his wife at all," another muttered.

"Listen to me, motherfuckers," Candy hissed. "GET ME UP or I'll sue the entire state of Ohio."

"Yes, yes," Tim said, running in frantic circles around his *wife*. "She's allergic to asphalt. She could DIE!"

"I thought she was OCD," a confused officer said.

"I meant PTSD," Tim said. "I'm a little off at the moment due to my wife's knee bending the WRONG WAY! I can't be responsible for anything I say."

"Dyin'," Candy cried out. "I'm dyin' and it's your fault. Get those fuckers who went back inside and help me get my fat fuckin' ass up."

The cops looked at each other in confusion. One shrugged and the other turned back to the house. "Jack. Joe. Back out here. We need to get this woman on her feet, or at least her foot. ASAP."

Jack and Joe walked back over to the scene and all four tried to assess how to get Candy off the ground. While I wanted to watch the rest of the show, our cue had arrived and it was time to perform.

As we slipped into the house, I heard Candy griping about her *fuckin' doctor* who wanted her to get some exercise. She told the poor policemen that she was going to sue the shit out of her doctor after she sued the shit out of the Ohio State Police if they didn't get her up off the ground before she died of asphalt asphyxiation. Tim was shrieking suggestions at the cops and the cops were flummoxed.

"Candy was right," Tory whispered as we headed for the desk. "We had nothing to worry about. She's insane."

"Correct," I whispered back.

I was relieved that Agnes' body had been removed. It was difficult and heartbreaking to see her lifeless and slumped over her desk yesterday. I took a quick glance around to make sure Tim hadn't misjudged the number of officers in the house. So far, so good. The décor was kitschy and comfortable. It was done in bright florals mixed with lots of warm peaches and cream. It was welcoming and lovely... just like Agnes had been.

"Focus," Tory insisted as she began opening each drawer and going through the contents.

She was on the right side. I immediately went to the left. The top drawer was filled with pencils, pens, sticky notepads and candy. I grabbed an Almond Joy and put it into my pocket. It was my favorite. It didn't surprise me that my buddy Agnes loved them too.

I glanced over at Tory. "Are we capable of leaving fingerprints?"

"Good question. The answer is no," she replied.

I sighed with relief and went back to work. Being invisible had its perks.

The bottom drawer was loaded with folders, all labeled precisely in black ink. I was certain I'd hit paydirt. Agnes was anal much to my relief. I quickly flipped through the folders. Tax records, bills and other important documents were filed in alphabetical order, but no Shit Pile folder to be found.

"Not here," I ground out, feeling a little panicky.

"That's because it's here," Tory said, holding up the beige folder labeled Shit Pile.

I came so close to screaming with joy, I could taste it. It

was only Tory's hiss that made me swallow it back. "You sure there's only one Shit Pile folder?"

"Positive," she assured me.

She handed me the folder and I tucked it under my shirt and into my pants. Glancing down, I realized it was now as invisible as the rest of me. Win-win.

"You grabbed my ass, motherfucker," Candy shrieked from the street. "That's sexual harassment, copper."

"Wanda, darling," Tim cried out. "It's not his fault. Your ass is tremendous."

Amidst all the crazy, I giggled. Tim's double entendre wasn't lost on me.

"Sir," one of the cops said, sounding pissed off and out of breath. "I'm gonna need you to step back."

"So you can cop a feel of my ass again?" Candy Vargo shouted. "Cause if you do, I'm gonna grab your nuts."

"Wanda," Tim chastised her. "Defiling the testicles of a man of the law is illegal. Isn't that right, Officer Bob?"

"Umm... yes," Officer Bob said. "Ma'am, I'm not sure we can get you off of the ground. We're going to have to wait for the paramedics."

"Are you pussies?" Candy bellowed. "You're lookin' like pussies to me."

"Oh my God," Tory choked out on a laugh. "I think it's time to whistle."

"Past time," I agreed.

Without a second of hesitation, I whistled. Tory waved her hand. We were no longer invisible. I was tempted to ask why it was so excruciating to become invisible yet it was painless to reverse it. I'd hold that inquiry for another time.

It took one minute before a back-to-normal Candy Vargo and Tim appeared in a blast of shimmering orange dust. I crossed my fingers and hoped in that small amount of time that he'd wiped the shitshow from the cops' minds.

"You got the shit?" Candy demanded.

"We've got the shit," I replied.

Tim grinned. "We're out of here."

CHAPTER THREE

"WHAT THE FUCK IS THAT?" CANDY VARGO SHOUTED AS WE
all stared in shock and frustration at the notes Agnes had
left behind.

We'd transported back to Georgia with no issue. I'd
quickly spread the papers from the folder out on the
kitchen table. When I looked at them, I wanted to cry. They
were illegible.

Tim, Charlie and Heather examined the mess. The
tension in the kitchen was through the roof.

"Darlings," Dirk said, taking a peek over Heather's shoulder. "It looks like hieroglyphics. And while that's a specialty
of mine, I've never seen any quite like this."

"Where are Abby, Prue and Rafe?" I asked. Maybe they
could make sense of the nightmare.

"Upstairs with the ghosts," Heather said as she sprinted
out of the room to get them.

"Bring Gram down too," I shouted after her. Gram was

closer to Agnes' age than I was. Maybe she knew what the disaster on the pages meant. It was a long shot, but what in my life wasn't recently? The person I really wanted was Jennifer. My dear friend knew more random facts and crap than most people, but she was at my father's former home that now belonged to Candy Vargo with Missy, June, Amelia and the other three wonderful Four Horsemen of the Apocalypse—Willy, Fred and Carl. They were protecting my baby, Alana Catherine. Since Micky Muggles could take on the visage of anyone, we weren't taking any chances with my child.

"Will do," she called out.

Tim was frantically typing away on his laptop computer. Candy had punched a hole in the wall and the rest of us just stared in dismay at the contents of the folder.

The need to run in the cold wind called to me. Running cleared my head, but there wasn't time. We had until sundown to figure out the spell and save Gideon, Gabe, Zander, Catriona and Zadkiel from Micky Muggles warped plans.

"Howdy, kiddies," Gram sang as she floated into the room with Rafe, Gabby and Prue on her tail. Heather was with them and so was Mr. Jackson. "What seems to be the problem, Daisy girl?"

Mr. Jackson was a ghost living in residence right now. I hadn't had time to help any of my deceased squatters lately and hoped he wasn't in great need. It would have to wait. He was a sweet gentleman who must have been in his eighties when he'd died. He was missing his left foot and half of the top of his head, but he had an irresistible smile that warmed a room. He also loved knock-knock jokes. I wasn't sure why he was here, but I didn't make him leave. Right now, I'd take any help I could get.

I pointed at the papers on the table. "Gram, do you know what that writing is? Have you seen anything like it before?" I held my breath and waited.

Gram floated above the papers and studied them. Mr. Jackson floated right next to her.

"Can't rightly say I do or have," Gram said, getting closer to the scribbles on the yellow legal pad sheets of paper. "Looks like a bunch of squiggly lines to me."

"Iiiiah dooooooooah!" Mr. Jackson said doing a few flips and losing his left arm in the process.

Grabbing a tube of superglue from the drawer, I gently pulled the ghost out of the air and seated him on a chair. Sometimes my hands when right through the ghosts. Sometimes, like now, they were corporeal, and I could touch them. I pushed down my excitement and kept my voice steady and calm. My instinct was to scream with joy, but I didn't want to scare Mr. Jackson. If he could read the doodles on the paper, we were home free—or at least partially. Granted, he was difficult to understand, but it was better than nothing.

I smiled at the adorable ghost while gluing his arm back on. "Can you tell me what it says, Mr. Jackson?"

He shook his head. "Nooooah."

My excitement plummeted and I felt faint. "Are you sure?" I pressed, holding it together by a thread.

"Suuurah," he said with a warm smile as he tested out his repaired appendage.

"Askin' the wrong question, fucker," Candy Vargo said, with six toothpicks in her mouth.

My frustrated gaze snapped to her. "Do you have the right question?"

"Maybe," she replied and took a seat next to Mr. Jackson. "Alrighty fucker, I know you can't read that crap, but do you know what kind of crap it is?"

I rolled my eyes and hoped Mr. Jackson didn't get upset at being called a fucker. Candy's people skills sucked. Thankfully, the silly man giggled.

"Candy Vargo," Gram warned, wagging a transparent finger in her face. "I'm fixin' to wash your nasty mouth out with soap!"

Candy blanched. Gram might be dead, but she was still in charge. Candy loved my grandmother and she loved her right back. Gram's mission was to teach Candy some manners. She had her work cut out for her.

"Sorry about that," Candy told Mr. Jackson. "Lemme rephrase. So... dead guy, can you tell me what the hell those fuckin' squiggles are? Not what they mean, but what the fuck they are?" She glanced over at Gram who was shaking her head. "Better?"

"Not much, but at least you didn't call Mr. Jackson the f-bomb again," Gram muttered. "Bless your heart, Candy Vargo. Sometimes the porch light is on, but there just ain't nobody home."

Candy grinned and took Gram's words as a sign of approval. Candy was an idiot.

"Plaaayah gaaameah?" Mr. Jackson asked quivering with excitement.

Candy looked like she was about to punch him. I quickly wedged myself between them. I knew her fist would go right through the ghost, but it was some serious bad manners to punch a nice old man—even a dead one. Upsetting him wasn't in the game plan. Apparently, playing a game was...

"Yes," I told him quickly. "If we play a game, will you tell us what the scribbles are?"

"Yausssss!"

Inhaling deeply to stay calm, I shoved Candy out of the chair and seated myself next to the ghost. "Knock-knock jokes?"

"Yaussss! Knooockha-knooockha."

"Who's there?" I asked.

He bounced with excitement. "Saaaaysssss."

"Says who?"

"Saaaaysssss meeeeeah!"

"Good one, Mr. Jackson," Gram said, patting the old man's back.

The sweet ghost laughed with delight. The sound was alarming—kind of like a death rattle, but I was used to it now. The joy of my dead guests was my joy too.

"Knooockha-knooockha."

I was all in. There was no other choice. "Who's there?"

"Coooowah saaaayssss," he replied with a grin that was macabre since he was missing half his head.

"Cow says who?"

"Naawwwooo," he yelled. "Coooowah saaaaysssss mooooooooooooo."

I laughed. I knew it was coming, but his silliness was contagious. "You got me."

"Laaasssstah oonneah," he told me. "Knooockha-knooockha."

I crossed my fingers and hoped that the answer I was looking for was coming. "Who's there?"

"Leeeeenaaah," he said.

"Leena who?"

All eyes were on Mr. Jackson along with all our hopes.

"Leeeeenaaah innnnnn aaah lllittlleee clooooserah aaandah Iiiiiii willllah teeeeelllah yooouah!"

I leaned in. My heart pounded loudly in my chest. If Mr. Jackson could shed some light on the strange markings, we weren't at the goal line, but we were closer. What I wanted more than taking my next breath was to hold Gideon in my arms and hear his laugh. I wanted both Gideon and our baby back home where they belonged... and I'd go to the ends of the world and back to make it happen.

"Ssshoooorttah-haaaandah," the kind ghost whispered.

"Shorthand?" I repeated as Tim slapped himself in the head.

"Oh my goodness, I should have recognized that," he lamented.

"Ssshoooorttah-haaaandah," Mr. Jackson repeated with a nod of his partial head.

"Dead fucker for the win!" Candy shouted and offered Mr. Jackson a toothpick.

He politely declined. The specter had much better manners than the Keeper of Fate.

"We need to find someone who can decipher shorthand," Charlie said, nodding his thanks to Mr. Jackson.

Tim was back on the computer typing like a madman. "I can learn it," he said. "But it might take a few hours. I'm fluent in most languages, but unfortunately not shorthand."

"I might be able to learn it as well," Dirk added while applying a shiny new coat of red lipstick. "But like Tim, it would take me the better part of the day."

"We don't have time for that," I said, pinching the bridge of my nose. My impending freakout was close.

"What about an app?" Heather asked. "Are there any online shorthand translators?"

Tim's fingers moved swiftly across the keys. "There are, but it looks tedious and time consuming. However, I'm downloading several now."

Gram scratched her head and groaned. "I'm thinkin' I might know a few gals who can read shorthand. The three of 'em are meaner than a wet panther and make my rump itch, but I'm pretty sure they used to be stenographers back in the day."

"Local?" Charlie asked.

Gram nodded. Her lips were pinched—a clear sign that she didn't like the shorthand reading ladies. It didn't matter. We were desperate.

"Who are they?" I asked.

Gram floated over and cupped my cheek with her papery hand. "They're the kind of gals who can kiss my go-to-hell."

"Not what I asked," I said with a smile as I placed my hand over hers. I thanked my lucky stars every day that she was still here with me. I knew that eventually she'd have to move on, but I wanted that day to be very far in the future.

"I know, girlie," she said with a chuckle then glanced around at the group. "Y'all know the Gladiolas?"

"The ladies club?" Heather asked, sounding stressed.

"Yep," Gram answered.

The local ladies club—The Gladiolas—maintained the flowerbeds in the park and other public areas in our small town. Normally, the ladies did more gossiping than gardening, but the old gals definitely had green thumbs. The gardens in our town were lovely.

Candy choked on her toothpick. Tim slapped her on the back and she spit it across the room. "Which ones?" Candy demanded.

"Well, now," Gram said. "I hesitate to call 'em ladies, but it's the three known as the Karens."

I was confused. All of the geriatric women in the Gladiolas were what I would call entitled pains in the butt, but I didn't recall any of them being named Karen.

"Wait. They're all named Karen?" I asked.

"Nah," Gram said. "That's just the nickname everyone calls 'em behind their backs since they're such nasty old biddies."

"Got it." I didn't care if they were spiteful, nasty abominations. I needed someone to read the scribble. The lives of those I loved were at stake. "What are their names?"

"Dimple, Jolly Sue and Lura Belle," she answered.

I didn't personally know the ladies. I knew who they were—everyone did. And everyone gave them a wide berth. All three were kind of beady-eyed and mean.

"Motherfucker," Candy bellowed as she punched the air with her fist and incinerated my toaster.

At least it wasn't the coffee pot. I would have retaliated if she'd messed with my favorite caffeine source.

Glancing around the room, I realized Charlie, Heather, Candy and Tim had paled considerably. Dirk, Tory, Rafe, Prue and Abby were fine. Charlie, Heather, Tim and Candy had all resided here in our sleepy town much longer than the others. Apparently, they knew Dimple, Jolly Sue and Lura Belle... and what they knew obviously wasn't good.

I didn't care. Dealing with three unpleasant humans for an hour or two wasn't the worst thing that could happen. If the information gleaned was weird or damning, Tim could wipe their minds like he'd done with the cops in Ohio.

"I don't see an issue," I said. "Who cares if they're entitled biddies? I certainly don't."

Heather cleared her throat then cleared it again. That didn't bode well. My sister was the most level headed woman I knew. "Do you know what Nephilim are?"

"Oh dear," Dirk said, fanning himself with his boa.

Dirk was one of the Four Horsemen of the Apocalypse and represented Death. The fact that he was unnerved made me a bit panicky. He was a badass in a dress and wasn't alarmed by much.

"Shit," Prue said.

"Double," Abby agreed.

"There are Nephilim here?" Rafe asked, appalled.

"Sure as hell are," Candy told him.

I blew out a long slow breath. "I don't know what Nephilim are."

"Cause she ain't read the Bible," Candy Vargo commented.

I wanted to electrocute her. I didn't. The payback wouldn't be worth it.

"Daisy's knowledge of the Bible is irrelevant," Tory said in a flat tone. "The book doesn't get Nephilim correct anyway."

"Fine point, well made," Tim agreed. He was still rather green around the gills, but no longer looked as if he was going to pass out. "A Nephilim is the result of an Angel breeding with a human."

I squinted at him. I was wildly unsure why a Nephilim was a bad thing... considering I was one. "Umm... my dad was an Angel and my mom was human," I reminded everyone.

"Not all Nephilim are shitasses," Candy Vargo said. "And you're much more than a common Nephilim. You're the Death Counselor and the Angel of Mercy. You're Immortal for fuck's sake."

I was so confused. "So most Nephilim aren't Immortal?"

Charlie shook his head. "No. They have a longer life span than a human, but they're not Immortal."

"Which is only one of the reasons they're pissed off," Heather chimed in. "Dimple, Jolly Sue and Lura Belle are the worst of the bunch. They have very little magic, but what they do have they've honed well."

"Can we be a little more specific here?" I asked, twisting my hair in my fingers and doing my best not to walk outside and blow a crater in my front yard. As of late, I'd realized that property destruction was therapeutic.

However, we were on a mission with devastating results if we didn't succeed. Craters would have to wait.

Charlie sighed and sat down. "They drove your father crazy," he admitted. "Michael threatened to banish them from here, but in the end let them stay... as long as they behaved."

"What can they do?" I pressed. All of the information was interesting in an off-putting way, but I needed hard facts. I didn't know how to deal with or fight something vague.

"Who wants to field this one?" Charlie inquired. "Not sure I can be objective."

"I'll do it," Candy announced.

"Nope," Heather said quickly. "I say Tim explains. He's the nicest and most diplomatic of all of us."

Tim blushed and smiled sheepishly. "Thank you, friend."

"Welcome," Heather replied.

"Alrighty then," Tim said, wringing his hands and doing his best to keep his expression neutral. "Let's start with Dimple."

"Don't you mean gaping jackhole of a bitch?" Candy Vargo inserted.

Tim ignored her and went on. "While being rude and unpleasant isn't technically a crime, Dimple is somewhat next level. If she chooses, she can make a person have bad luck."

"Very fuckin' bad luck," Candy Vargo said.

I closed my eyes and shook my head. "You mean she can make people trip on the sidewalk at will? Stuff like that?"

"Umm... sure," Tim said. "But Dimple prefers causing

people to get struck by lightning, go bankrupt, get hit by busses, slide on the ice and break their leg, you know... a little more next level."

"What the fu..." I swallowed the bad word since Gram was present, but old Dimple was a walking profanity. Her behavior wasn't even remotely angelic. Although, some of the Angels I'd met and dealt with were worse than the Demons I knew. Heck, Gideon was a Demon and was the finest person I'd ever met—loyal, loving and fair.

"The only thing off limits is death," Heather said flatly. "Do you recall when George Nugal had the car accident where he plowed into Coco's Cooky Crafts and obliterated the entire shop?"

My mouth fell open and I nodded.

"Dimple," Heather said with a disgusted shake of her head. "Apparently, she had the hots for Old Man Nugal and he sat next to Coco at bingo night."

"Was anyone actually hurt?" I asked, unable to remember all the details.

"No," Charlie said. "However, Coco's shop was destroyed and neither her insurance nor George Nugal's would pay."

"Because of something Dimple did?" I asked.

"Bingo—pun intended," Tim said with a wince.

"Mean," Gram huffed. "Even sayin' her name sticks in my throat like hair in a dang biscuit."

Gram's analogies were always colorful. I would have laughed if what we were talking about wasn't so disturbing.

"Hair from an asshole," Candy Vargo added. "I'd call it a butt biscuit."

The visual Gram had created was bad enough. Candy had just upped the level of gross.

"You can stop right there," Heather warned Candy.

"Just tellin' it like it is," Candy shot back.

"What about Jolly Sue?" I asked, not wanting to witness a smackdown between Candy and Heather. They were both insanely powerful. Plus, there was no time for infighting.

"Jolly Sue has the ability to make someone act on their worst impulses. Quite dreadful," Tim shared.

"Examples?" I asked. If I was going to deal with them, I needed to know exactly what I was dealing with.

Tim sighed. "She can exacerbate someone's road rage, with a wiggle of her finger. There was a legendary fist fight at the Piggly Wiggly over lunchmeat a year ago. It happened between two of the kindest men in our community. Hooter Smith lost his mind that Jimmy Wilson got the last of the honey ham. Instead of asking Irma if there was more in the back—which there was, he beat the tar out of Jimmy."

"From what I heard, Jolly Sue just stood there and laughed," Candy said with a growl. "I wasn't at work that day. If I had been, I woulda blasted her sorry ass and made her eat a whole fuckin' ham."

Honestly, I didn't find Candy's brand of justice for Jolly Sue all that bad.

"And Lura Belle?" I asked.

"Lura Belle has the ability to make someone see the worst in themselves," Tim said. "It's a truly evil power."

"That just chaps my ass," Gram muttered.

Candy Vargo was steaming. "Y'all know that nice gal Donette and her sister, Hazelene?"

"I do," I said. They were two older spinsters who crocheted. Word on the street was that they crocheted sleeves for sex toys and ran a little online business, but I didn't judge. To each his own. I aided dead people and had no room to talk about strange jobs.

"Well, that fucker Lura Belle knew they were insecure about crocheting dildo covers so she took an anonymous ad out in the paper tellin' the town what the nutbags were up to. They got banned from the Gladiolas over it. Donnette thought about offin' herself. Hazelene almost succeeded."

"Oh my God," I said. "The ad was anonymous. How do you know it was Lura Belle?"

Candy rolled her eyes. "I own the fuckin' paper."

And the weird kept getting weirder. I was sure I didn't know even half of the stuff about the people I called my friends. Granted, they were older than dirt, but still…

"Yeppers," Candy said, biting down so hard she split the toothpick she was chewing on in half. "I inserted myself into that bullshit. Donnette and Hazelene are right nice humans. Always say hi at the Piggly Wiggly and they made scarfs and hats for my foster kids. I don't like it when assholes fuck with nice people."

I winced a little. "What did you do?"

"Actually," Tim chimed in, patting Candy on the back. "She didn't dismember anyone. I was quite proud of her for her restraint. Instead, she found a company that wanted to buy Donnette and Hazelene's designs for vibrator covers. Made it look like they'd seen the ad in the paper and approached them for the patent!"

"Hell to the yes," Candy said with a wide grin. "Them

crazy ladies got two million fuckin' dollars for the rights. Lura Belle about crapped her pants."

"Two point five million," Heather corrected Candy with an even wider grin. "I represented them in the transaction."

I might not know all the ins and outs of my chosen and blood family, but I knew they had huge hearts and were hella smart.

"Those Nephilim are just dreadful," Dirk fretted, still applying lipstick. He now looked like he was bleeding from the mouth. "Who on Earth gave them their powers?"

"Zadkiel," Charlie said flatly. "It makes sense since he sired them."

Prue, Abby and Rafe hissed with displeasure. Zadkiel had terrorized them for thousands of years. Their hatred of him was vicious and real.

"Shut the front door," I choked out. "He has children? That heartless asshole is a freaking father?"

Candy blew a raspberry. "More like a sperm donor," she spat. "Gonna say part of the old bitches' problems are daddy issues. That fucker probably has thousands of nasty bastards all over the world."

Digesting the toxic news was mind-boggling, but not that surprising. Zadkiel may have been a good man millions of years ago, but in the end, he'd left a legacy of horror behind.

"Let me get this straight," I said, pacing the kitchen to keep my thoughts in order. "Dimple creates bad luck. Jolly Sue makes people act on their worst impulses and Lura Belle makes people see the worst in themselves?"

"Correct," Charlie said.

"This town is nuts," Tory muttered. "It's like a hot bed for Immortal and partially magical whackjobs."

Tim smiled at Tory. "True," he told her. "This is a very special place indeed. It sits on ley lines and is the most accessible location in the world for portals into the Darkness and the Light."

Since that was the case, I briefly wondered if there was anyone else I'd known my whole life who wasn't human. That was a conversation for another time. Right now, the subject was Nephilim.

"Can they mess with Immortals?" I questioned. I was hanging on by a thread. I didn't need any extra help with bad luck, poor impulses or seeing the worst in myself. My plate was already full.

"No," Heather said. "They try, but it usually backfires."

"Can they see ghosts?" I asked.

"Not sure," Charlie said. "Best to not test that. The less they know about our lives the better. Along with the fact that the ghosts were once human, I'm unsure if what they do could affect them in death."

"Good to know," I said, pulling out my phone. "Does anyone have their phone numbers?"

"Ohhh, darling," Dirk said, handing me his tube of lipstick. "We're really going to ask them for help?"

I put some lipstick on and immediately felt better. Who knew red lips were a mood booster? "We don't have a choice. We need the spell and they can read shorthand."

"I hate them fuckers, but I think Daisy is right." Candy Vargo began to glow an eerie bluish color. "Well, crap. My butt cheek is itching,"

"Oh my!" Tim said, hopping to his feet and gently leading Candy to a chair.

"Back up everyone," Charlie advised as he helped Tim.

Magic filled the room quickly and made it a little difficult to breathe. Candy's hair blew around her head and the box of toothpicks she held fell to the floor and scattered. She began to chant in a haunting melody.

I'd seen this happen several times. I wasn't surprised or alarmed when her eyes rolled back and her body went limp. I hoped to hell and back it was a message from Gideon. When an Immortal needed assistance or wanted to send a message, Candy's left butt cheek tingled and she went into a trance.

"Whhaaaatssssah haaappeeeeeningah?" Mr. Jackson asked, worried.

"It's fine," I assured him. "Candy gets ass messages."

"Deeeeliightfuuulllll," he said.

"Remains to be seen," Tory muttered.

Candy began to speak. Her voice was low and ominous. It was disconcerting, but I knew she wasn't dying. A sharp chilly wind blew through the house and I quickly grabbed my coffee maker so it didn't crash to the ground. The blender didn't make it. I didn't care. Coffee was way more important than smoothies in my world. The Keeper of Fate convulsed then stilled like she was dead.

"The one who giveth, can taketh away," she said in a monotone. "Or if denied, the next one can."

We all waited for more.

There was no more.

Shimmering orange crystals rained down from the

ceiling and covered every surface of the kitchen. Candy Vargo passed out. Heather gathered Agnes' papers and put them back in the folder. Charlie and Tim carefully picked Candy up and laid her on the kitchen table. Tory grabbed some dishtowels and put them under Candy's head. Her act of pretending not to care wasn't working.

Inhaling deeply, I put the coffee maker back on the counter and brushed some of the crystals off my clothes. "Does anyone know what she meant?"

My answer was silence.

All of the messages we'd received in the past from Candy's ass had been cryptic. It didn't seem like a message Gideon or Gabe would send. While I didn't know Zander well, it didn't sound like him. Could it be his sister Catriona? Maybe, but probably not. She didn't know any of us. Or could it have been The Collector trying to throw us off the track?

I shook my head. The message didn't sound like Micky Muggles, and I was betting he was too much of a narcissist to disguise his voice.

There was no doubt the message was important, whoever sent it. I would figure it out. Whatever it took. Period.

"Here are the numbers for the Nephilim," Tim said handing me a piece of paper.

I stared at the numbers for a moment, then pulled out my phone. The clock was ticking and we needed answers. Now. I was going to get them and I was going to win.

There was no other option.

CHAPTER FOUR

OCCASIONALLY, YOU MEET PEOPLE AND YOU KNOW FROM THE very first instant you interact that you would happily spend the rest of your life never crossing their paths again. The 'Karens' fell into that category.

After calling each of them multiple times and get hung up on just as many times, I was ready to explode on their half-angel asses. It took Candy Vargo going into town and threatening to do a massive expose in the newspaper on all the illegal and shitty activities they'd participated in over the years to get them to come to my house.

Dimple, Jolly Sue and Lura Belle had come unwillingly, but they were here. Now the trick remained to get them to read the shorthand without anyone killing them. That was going to be a challenge. They were argumentative, rude and condescending—a winning combination.

"So," I said, trying not to sigh loudly, groan or throat-punch any of them. "As I've requested for the last twenty minutes, I would greatly appreciate it if you could read the shorthand to us. You'll be compensated dearly. You have my word."

Dimple, Jolly Sue and Lura Belle were seated on the couch near the fireplace. Tim, Heather and I were on the couch across from them. Charlie, Candy and Tory stood behind us. Agnes' Shit Pile folder lay on the coffee table between us. Our guests sat ramrod straight with their hands clasped primly in their laps and stared daggers at us.

"My word is good," I added.

The trio huffed and rolled their eyes. Before they'd arrived, we'd sent the ghosts upstairs. Rafe, Prue, Abby and Dirk had gone with them. We'd kept our group smallish. The 'Karens' knew everyone present except Tory. The familiarity and their knowledge of who we were in the Immortal world didn't seem to be helping. Their lack of fear wasn't surprising considering their sperm donor was Zadkiel. The Angel's reckless disregard for any kind of decent humanity had clearly been passed down.

Dimple glanced around my great room and wrinkled her nose. "I cannot be expected to buy sheets for the bed you made," she snapped. "Plus, the *word* of an Immortal is useless."

Candy Vargo raised a brow and Dimple shrunk a bit. "Some fuckers drink from the well of knowledge. Some just rinse and spit. You're a spitter."

"And you are an artless, beef-witted, bawdy canker-blossom," Dimple retorted, looking down her nose at the Keeper of Fate.

She wasn't smart to smack talk Candy. Dimple also

seemed to have an affinity for insults dating back to the 1600s.

If I had to describe Dimple, the term cat-butt face came to mind. Her wrinkled lips were pursed into a permanent O —hence the cat-butt reference. All three of them had clearly dipped from the same gene pool and had similar features. The only attractive thing about them were their cornflower blue eyes. Other than that, their attitudes destroyed any prettiness to be found. Not that they were ugly—quite the opposite. All three were very well preserved and expertly coiffed seventy-somethings, dressed conservatively and expensively in what I recognized as Chanel. I was more of a sweatpants gal and I liked it that way.

Of course, seventy was a guess. In reality, I had no clue how many years they'd lived.

"I'd suggest you read the shorthand," Charlie said in a tone that should have made them run for the hills.

They just laughed. Again, they reminded me of Zadkiel. It made my stomach churn.

"I'd suggest that you take your opinion and shove it up your mangled, clay-brained, loggerheaded clotpole," Jolly Sue snapped at Charlie. "You Immortals believe you're so high and mighty. I'm here to tell you that you're impertinent, beslubbering, hedge pigs."

Tory's brows shot up and she choked back a laugh. If the situation wasn't dire their vernacular might have been amusing.

Tim gave it a shot. "Ladies…"

"And he uses that term fuckin' loosely," Candy chimed in.

He didn't acknowledge his BFFs comment. "If you would be so kind as to help us, we could discuss a compensation that doesn't consist of money."

I didn't like the direction he was going, but desperate times called for possibly stupid measures. I couldn't even begin to imagine what the nasty women would want. However, they perked up at the offer.

Crap.

"You," Lura Sue said, pointing her sharply manicured finger at me.

"I have a name," I told her coolly.

"Of course, you do," she sneered. "How did a haggard, fat-kidneyed, nut-hook like you become the new Angel of Mercy? You're just a Nephilim."

Lura Belle along with her nasty cohorts seemed to love Shakespearian insults. Honestly, it was so absurd it made me want to laugh... so I did. My amusement went over like a lead balloon. All three Nephilim hissed. I didn't care. If they wanted to play games, we'd try the shorthand translator app that Tim had downloaded. I was beginning to believe that bargaining with them could be a grave mistake.

"She was never *just* a Nephilim, you fuckers," Candy growled. "Daisy's the Death Counselor as well. So put that in your pipe and smoke it, then shove it up your saggy asses."

I held up a hand to Candy to indicate I had this under control. While I always appreciated backup, Candy's brand was offensive. Gram had always said you could catch more bees with honey. I was pretty sure that wasn't going to work in this situation, but I'd try.

"I understand that you're…" I began.

"SHUT UP!" Jolly Sue bellowed. "You're not in charge. You want something that we have. Guess the ball is in our court this time."

Dimple smiled. It was hideous and filled with fury. "We are making the terms here."

"And if you don't accept, we'll walk," Lura Belle added, baring her teeth.

I gave Lura Belle a hard glare that made her gulp. My fingers began to spark and my hair blew wildly around my head. My furbabies Donna and Karen growled at the rude women and the tense mood in the room became hostile.

"Listen to me," I ground out. "If you're not going to read the shorthand you can leave. And by leave, I mean leave this town. Forever. My father might have been tolerant of you, but I have no patience for assholes who take pride and joy in other people's suffering. Women like you make me sick. You're as revolting as the abhorrent low-life who sired you."

They were wildly taken aback and huddled together whispering amongst themselves. Dimple kept shaking her fist at me until Candy shot a bolt of lightning that came very close to setting the trio ablaze. Their infighting escalated. When Dimple slapped Jolly Sue in the face, I was shocked. Lura Belle growled at the others like an animal and they both froze. The Nephilim were nucking futs as Gram used to say when she was truly pissed. Lura Belle pointed to the corner. Dimple and Jolly Sue walked over to it and stood there.

She'd put her sisters in timeout. Bizarre didn't even begin to describe their behavior.

The obvious leader of the three turned and glared at me. "Tell us why the shorthand is important."

I glanced over at Tim. I didn't care that the Nephilim could hear me. "Can you wipe their minds?"

The appalled gasps from the Karens were expected. Tim's answer was not.

"No," he replied. "It only works on humans—full humans."

Running my hands through my hair, I did my best to tamp back all the magic that was begging to be released and expended by electrocuting the old biddies. I had no clue if they could survive a magical attack. Ending them for real wasn't on the agenda. What might feel satisfying in the moment was beyond wrong in the long game. Checking my watch, I felt my panic bubble up. It was only ten in the morning, but time moved quickly when you didn't want it to.

Another tactic was necessary.

"Karens in the corner," I said in a brook-no-bullshit tone. "Go back to the couch and sit down."

They really wanted to defy me, but I was sparking and glowing. I was aware that my eyes had turned a blinding gold since the room was awash in a yellow haze. The gals were smart not to test me. I wasn't playing around.

"Do you enjoy living?" I asked, casually.

Dimple's eyes narrowed to slits. "Are you threatening us?"

"Not at all," I told her. "The shorthand needs to be read to reverse an imbalance that could lead to Armageddon."

Jolly Sue sneered. "And I have a bridge for sale, you, cockered, weedy, strumpet."

I winked at her. She had no clue what to do with that. Walking to the bottom of the stairs, I cupped my hands around my mouth and called out. "Death," I yelled. "Would you mind coming down and greeting a few of our guests? They don't believe you're here."

"Full on badass, darling?" Dirk called back.

"Full on badass," I confirmed.

"Hell to the yes," Candy Vargo said with a laugh.

The Karens grew uncomfortable. I didn't care. What I needed was for them to read the papers then get the heck out of my house. I'd sage the dang place when all of this was over. My BFF Missy sold sage in her bookshop. I planned to buy her out of her supply. Not only had the old women brought shitty karma into my home, but Micky Muggles and Zadkiel had been here too. The need for a cleanse was real.

"I'm ready for my entrance, darlings!" Dirk squealed. "Here I come, ready or not!"

What I expected was for Dirk to walk down the stairs with horns on fire, and fangs and claws out. Of course, nothing ever happens as expected. My dear friend was a drag queen. He never did anything half-assed.

Yes, his horns were on fire. Yes, his fangs and claws were out. Yes, he was terrifying and personified death and then some. Yes, flames shot from his mouth, nostrils and ears. Yes, he wore a beaded red ballgown. However, the Horseman of the Apocalypse known as Death didn't walk down the stairs. He rode a massive horse, knocking down the railing and causing all the pictures to fall off the walls. Death's enormous steed was an ashen pale green.

Charlie chuckled. Tory joined him. Heather grinned from ear to ear. Candy Vargo did a little jig and Tim just smiled and shook his head. My dogs wagged their tails with gusto. The Karens, on the other hand, had a very different reaction. They screamed in horror and dropped to their knees.

"You rang?" Dirk demanded of the trio on the ground. He dismounted and glared at them. He had no clue what was actually going on, but my drag queen buddy was no one's dummy.

"No," Dimple said in a shaky voice. "Go back to where you came from, Hell spawn."

"Be banished," Jolly Sue shouted.

Dirk rolled his eyes. "Rude."

Lura Belle got to her feet shakily. "Our apologies," she choked out, trembling from head to toe. Her sisters began to protest and she slapped both of them silly. "We didn't realize the gravity of the situation. We will read the shorthand."

"Excellent," Dirk said, patting his equine sidekick, then squatting down and giving the dogs a quick belly scratch. "I shall go back upstairs and continue to view *The Price is Right*. It's almost time for the big showcase."

Dirk hopped back up on his horse as Dimple, Jolly Sue and Lura Belle exchanged confused glances. I did suppose it was odd to think Death enjoyed *The Price Is Right*, but Gram had gotten all four queens hooked on it.

"Let this be a warning," Dirk said in a tone that made the

hair on the back of my neck stand up. He looked over his shoulder at the Karens as he slowly began to guide his horse back up the stairs. "If you lie about what's on the papers, your end will be *very* unpleasant... if you know what I mean."

Dimple, Jolly Sue and Lura Belle nodded spastically as my dogs happily trotted after him.

He laughed manically and rode back up to the second floor. My house was a wreck—didn't matter. Houses were things and could be replaced. Gideon couldn't be replaced.

"Shall we get started, fuckers?" Candy Vargo inquired, as she opened the folder and placed the individual pages on the coffee table.

Again, the Karens nodded frantically.

We'd retrieved the Shit Pile folder. We'd convinced the Nephilim to read the contents. We were about to learn the spell.

Three parts down.

So many more to go.

CHAPTER FIVE

DIMPLE, JOLLY SUE AND LURA BELLE WERE SCANDALIZED BY the words on the pages. All three were a deep and unattractive shade of red. There were fifteen pages total and each of the women had taken five to decipher. Tim was poised over his laptop computer ready to take notes. Heather had set her phone to record. Candy stood over the Nephilim after a warning she would tear them limb from limb then shove their dismembered appendages up their asses if they tried to destroy Agnes' notes. I was glad she said something. It was far harsher than anything I would have said, but the Nephilim seemed to understand anger and violence.

A part of me felt sorry for the trio of biddies. With Zadkiel as their sperm donor, they really didn't stand much of a chance. He'd given them disastrous gifts. The original Angel of Mercy was a sadistic man.

Dimple slapped the pages down on the coffee table and glared at me. Her cat-butt face was in full force. "I detect a distinct lack of Southern hospitality in this house, you pribbling lewdster," she snapped, crossing her arms over her chest.

I blanched in embarrassment. Aside from the ridiculous names she'd just hurled at me, Dimple was correct. I'd completely forgotten my manners. Gram wouldn't be pleased. Even though my guests were hideous, they were still guests. I'd been raised far better than to forget to offer refreshment. Manners were in my Southern DNA. Although, I did cut myself a break. At sundown today I could lose my world. Saving Gideon and Gabe along with the others was my goal. I needed the Karens' knowledge of shorthand to achieve it.

Immediately standing up, I clasped my hands in front of me contritely. "My apologies. Can I offer you umm… ladies something to drink or a snack?"

Jolly Sue answered for the group. "We'd like some sweet tea and hot biscuits with peas."

"I'm sorry, what?" I asked, sure I'd heard her wrong.

"Sweet tea," she ground out. "And hot biscuits with peas."

I glanced over at Heather in a panic. First off, the combo was weird and gross. Secondly, I was pretty sure I didn't have biscuits or peas in the pantry. My sister just shrugged and wrinkled her nose.

"I've got this," Tim said, getting to his feet. "Hot biscuits with peas coming right up."

Tim couldn't cook to save his life. It was going to end badly. My buddy's idea of a gourmet dish was combining cocktail weenies, fruit and crackers with every condiment known to man then baking it. His culinary creations smelled like rotting trash. He usually added some kind of mystery meat. I was delighted to be a vegetarian.

"Tim," I called after him as he made his way to the kitchen. "Not sure I have the right ingredients."

"Not to worry," he assured me. "I grocery shopped for you a few days ago. Biscuits, creamed peas, prunes, spam and salted peanuts are components in the dish I was going to prepare for lunch. All's good."

I gagged softly. Being rude to Tim was never going to happen, no matter how nasty his cooking might be. Besides, his horrid taste in food was a big win right now.

"Don't forget the sweet tea," Lura Belle grumbled.

"My God," Jolly Sue huffed, shaking the papers above her head. "All five of these pages wax poetic about dragon genitalia. I've never heard so many terms for a male member in my life. Appalling."

"Is there any fornication? Masturbation?" Candy leaned in. "Castration?" she asked hopefully.

"Umm… Candy," I said, pressing the bridge of my nose. "We're not looking for dragon sex or appendage dismemberment."

Candy Vargo pointed at me. "You don't know what you're missin', on both counts."

"I'm good with that," I replied as Dimple gasped and fanned herself with the papers.

"Is this some kind of joke?" she screeched, referring to whatever the heck was written in shorthand. "You've brought us over here to give us heart attacks, you gorbellied, malt-worm, flax-wench? I've never seen such filthy dreck in my life."

Candy began to glow. "You watch your mouth, Nephilim. You're privy to some of the greatest writin' known to fuckin' romance."

"Pun intended?" Tim asked, popping his head out of the kitchen with a wide grin.

Candy threw her head back and cackled. "Yep."

Lura Belle's lips had gone from cat-butt to a compressed thin line. "If you mewling maggot-pies are searching for directions on how to mount an erect dragon, you're out of luck. I refuse to read aloud the ins and outs of dragon banging."

"Oh my! Pun intended?" Tim inquired again, then went back to work on the hot biscuits and peas.

Lura Belle ignored him. The Nephilim had zero sense of humor. Granted, it was rather sophomoric.

"And this," Jolly Sue shouted, pointing to a bunch of squiggly lines. "It's dastardly."

"What is it?" I asked, hoping it was the spell.

She glared at the paper and read aloud in a clipped and disgusted tone. "The word *homeowner* has the word *meow* in the middle of it. Good luck ever pronouncing it the right way again. Ho-*meow*-ner."

"Vicious," Dimple said.

"Wicked," Lura Belle added. "I shall announce it at the next town hall meeting. If we're stuck with this diabolical knowledge, others must suffer as well."

Dimple giggled. It was actually kind of cute and was in stark juxtaposition to her dreadful demeanor. "Shall I phone Ruby Jewel and ruin her day? She's quite pompous about purchasing her new abode."

"Yesssss," the other two hissed with joy.

Ruby Jewel was ninety if she was a day. Buying a new home was a little odd at her age, but most of the inhabitants of this small town were strange.

"Pretty sure Ruby Jewel's dead," Candy chimed in.

Dimple gaped at Candy in surprise. "Are you serious?" she demanded.

Candy Vargo shrugged. "Heard it at the Piggly Wiggly last week."

Jolly Sue huffed, pulled out her phone, dialed then put it on speaker.

"Howdy," a voice yelled from the other side of the call.

It sounded very much like Ruby Jewel.

Jolly Sue sneered triumphantly. "Word on the street is that you're dead, you bootless, beetle-headed punkling."

"Not dead yet, you cow-patty, pea-eaten she-devil," Ruby Jewel shouted. "Heard you got false teeth!"

"Lies," Jolly Sue screamed as Dimple and Lura Belle's eyes grew huge confirming the news. "And just for your information, the word meow is smack in the middle of homeowner!"

"Alrighty then," Ruby Jewel—who was clearly hard of hearing bellowed. "I might have that stuck in my brain the rest of my years, but you're never gonna own a house, Jolly Sue. You're so poor, I heard you got a tumble weed for a pet."

"Well, I have never," Dimple gasped out.

"Is that you, Dimple?" Ruby Jewel yelled.

"Sure is," Candy Vargo confirmed.

Ruby Jewel was just getting started. "Dimple, you don't

know whether to scratch your bony ass or check the watch attached to your wrinkly age-spotted wrist! You might think the sun comes up to hear you crow, but you're wrong. Ain't no one likes you."

"Enough," Lura Belle snapped, horrified at the insults.

"Lura Belle?" Ruby Jewel hollered with a cackle. "Your brains rattle around like a BB in a boxcar. And before I go out and buy me a new couch for my brand-new house as a ho-meow-ner, I'll leave you dried up, prune eatin' biddies with a final thought. The word classlessness contains the word ass. Chew on that for a bit!"

On that serious burn, Ruby Jewel hung up. The Nephilim were speechless and pissed.

"Daaayum," Candy said with a chuckle. "I'm gonna have to take old Ruby Jewel out to lunch and learn me some new insults."

We were wasting time that we didn't have. I glanced over at Charlie. He nodded curtly. I wasn't sure if the man could read my face or my mind. It didn't matter.

"Be specific," he said. "Being cryptic won't work."

I almost laughed at the irony. Immortals were the most mysteriously enigmatic people I knew. I was the new kind of Immortal—blunt and to the point. Inhaling and feeling like I might implode, I pointed to the papers. "We're looking for a spell. Find the spell. My guess is that it has nothing to do with dragon fornication."

Dimple rolled her eyes. "It might have helped if you'd opened with that, you yeasty barnacle," she hissed. "I'll need to bleach my brain after this exercise in pornography."

"No worries," I said in a sugary Southern tone with a

blank expression. "If we don't find the spell, no one lives to see tomorrow. Your brain will be the least of your worries. My guess would be that where you'll be residing in your afterlife will be more of a concern."

Dimple, Jolly Sue and Lura Belle went as white as sheets.

I wasn't sure if what I'd said was accurate, but went with it. I'd heard enough about the entity, *the higher power*, to know that creating an imbalance within the Immortal world would not end well. Gideon and Gabe were integral to the balance. However, I'd been bluffing about not seeing tomorrow. I hoped to hell and back that my lie didn't become a truth.

Glancing over at Charlie, he squinted at me skeptically. Thankfully, he didn't call me out.

"Fine," Jolly Sue grumbled, scanning the pages. "Do you have any other clues that might help, you dankish, mammering wagtail?"

"It's a spell cast by a Dragon to create a parallel plane to hide his hoard, you impertinent, droning foot-licker," I answered much to her shocked surprise. My studies of Shakespeare back in college were coming in handy. My professor had been a huge fan of sixteenth century offensive language. "I need to get to that plane."

Dimple glanced at me sharply. "I thought this was fiction."

"The truth is always stranger than fiction," Tim said, holding a tray with piping hot biscuits, sweet tea and a bowl of creamed peas.

"It is fiction," I explained. "Dragons aren't real. Parallel planes and hoards are."

The trio exchanged loaded glances. While I was curious what they were thinking, it didn't matter. All I needed was the damned spell—damned being the operative word.

"I found something," Lura Belle said, looking smug. "But first we want more information."

I wanted to electrocute her. I didn't. The idiots were barely magical. Nothing they could do would harm me, my child or any of the people here. The only ones they could affect with their terrible gifts were humans and most likely other Nephilim.

"Who's the dragon? Metaphorically speaking?" she demanded.

"Not important," I replied. The less they knew the safer they would be. I might not like them, but they didn't need to be any more involved than they already were. It was too dangerous.

"What's in the hoard?" Dimple questioned.

"Again, not important," I replied tightly.

"Where is the hoard?" Jolly Sue questioned.

"Here," I told them. "In my home."

The Nephilim exchanged knowing looks. I felt my hands begin to spark dangerously and I shoved them into my pockets. My nerves were raw and they were treading on seriously thin ice. While not much happened in the Immortal world without reason, they were not Immortals. They were asses with nasty and weak powers bestowed upon them by their beast of a father.

Dimple took a biscuit and began to nibble on it. Jolly Sue poured peas all over hers and dug in. Lura Belle only ate the peas.

"Shall we strike a deal?" Lura Belle suggested once she stopped chewing.

"Are you shitting me?" I ground out.

The icky woman smirked. "I shit you not."

"Yes," Tory replied in a harsh tone.

I looked over at her in surprise. She hadn't said a word so far.

"State your terms," Tory said in an icy tone. "And then we shall state ours."

The *ladies* didn't like that, but they started it. Tory was going to finish it.

"Who are you?" Dimple asked warily.

Tory smiled. It was terrifying. "Someone who I'm sure you'll get to know at some point... soon."

"Sheee-ot," Candy Vargo said with a burst of laughter. "Y'all best stay on your toes."

The Nephilim whispered amongst themselves for a moment. Lura Belle—as usual—took the lead. "If we guess who the dragon is, you will tell us what's in the hoard."

The chances of that were slim to none.

"And if you get it wrong... you'll forfeit your lives," Tory said flatly. "Think hard if you want to play games with us. The consequences are non-negotiable."

I raised a brow. While I'd been bluffing earlier, I was positive Tory was not. She might deny loving Gabe, but her actions proved otherwise.

"Hold on," I said, approaching the old women. "Spell first. Guesses second. The stakes are too high."

Jolly Sue nodded primly. Tory's warning didn't sway

their decision to take a guess. Apparently, they were mean, stupid and had a death wish.

"Seems to be directions before the actual spell," Jolly Sue said, studying the page.

"All of it," I insisted. "Read all of it, please."

Tim was back at his computer. Heather aimed her phone toward the Nephilim. Charlie had pulled a pad of paper and a pen from his pocket and was ready to take notes. Tory was as still as a statue and listened. Candy Vargo chewed on a toothpick and kept her focus on the action. With all of us working together, there was little chance anything would be missed.

Jolly Sue picked up one of the pages. The Nephilim took a sip of sweet tea then cleared her throat. "To find the plane, one must break the chain. It must be broken by one of their own. The words have magic. They must be used before all becomes tragic. The key is to destroy the *catabibazon* to stop other hoards. In that place the enchantment is stored." She took another sip of tea and continued. "All good things come in three. If you plant the seed, it becomes a tree. To find the dragon, say the words. But be very careful when the worlds grow blurred... Draca. Dreki. Draco."

The house rumbled a bit on its foundation.

"Fuck," Candy Vargo yelled, pointing at Dimple, Jolly Sue and Lura Belle. "Don't say them words again."

"Agreed," I said, adding, "What the heck is a *catabibazon?*"

"A *catabibazon* is an old word that indicates an orbital node created by an inclined plane intersecting with an orbit," Charlie replied. "That's the only meaning I know."

"That's clear as mud." I felt even more confounded. "And explains nothing."

The Enforcer shrugged, took the papers away from the Nephilim then snapped his fingers. They disappeared in a blast of icy blue glitter. "The papers are safe," he assured me when he noticed my open-mouthed stare of horror. Charlie had gone all badass. His eyes sparked and he glowed. "We have what we need. I don't think the Nephilim are powerful enough to cast the spell, but no one says the words again until we're ready."

"Don't be so sure a Nephilim can't cast the spell," Dimple announced.

My gaze shot to hers. She had a smugly triumphant expression on her pinched face. My gut dropped. Was she actually Micky Muggles? Had he morphed into her?

"How could I be so damn careless?" I ground out. "Candy, drop a barrier around them. NOW."

The Keeper of Fate didn't hesitate. In less time than it took to exhale, the Nephilim were trapped in an enchanted bubble cage. If they were who they said they were, they wouldn't be able to get out. However, if one of them was Micky—meaning Micky had assumed one of the old gals' bodies... all bets were off.

None of them seemed concerned. They just kept eating their hot biscuits and peas. It was bizarre.

"Why?" Tory asked me.

"Because one of them might be the piece of shit that caused all of this," I replied.

"Any of us could be him," Tim pointed out.

He was correct.

Blowing up the house would be counterproductive. I really *really* wanted to. Instead, I pushed myself to be logical. Emotions were irrelevant in the situation. Who did I need other than myself? The question was premature. I had no clue who was the best to choose and assuming could end badly. "Tory, go invisible, hold onto my arm and don't let go."

Without a word, she did as asked. I felt her grip and sighed with relief.

There was no way Micky Muggles could go invisible. It took a very powerful Immortal to pull that trick. Hell, the *Dragoon* was barely able to withstand the beating Zander had given him, which was odd...

I wasn't sure how to test if my other friends were who I thought they were. How to keep all of us safe was important. Missing the clues seemed to be a character trait for me at this point. Micky Muggles was a master of deception. I'd seen it happen with my own eyes when he'd taken on the visage of Zander's sister, Catriona. That had ended tragically. There would be no repeat performance. Gideon, Gabe, Zander, Catriona and even Zadkiel's lives were at stake.

"Everyone else, leave," I instructed. "Please." If anyone refused, it would be suspect.

"Not so fast," Dimple yelled from within the bubble. "The dragon you're lookin' for is *not* Immortal."

I rolled my eyes and ignored her. Had Tim spiked the sweet tea?

"Listen to me, you churlish, frothy giglet," Dimple

shouted. "Micky Muggles is the dragon. That slimy asshole is a Nephilim—he's not Immortal."

Everyone froze. The accusation Dimple made didn't make sense. Micky Muggles had been around a very long time. Nephilim—while living longer than the normal lifespan of a human—couldn't survive for the thousands of years the mulleted-son-of-a-bitch had. However, the fact that she'd named him sent shivers up my spine.

"Impossible," Charlie ground out.

Jolly Sue stood up and shrugged her bony shoulders. "He doesn't have a footprint. Nephilim don't have footprints."

All Immortals had a magical footprint, so to speak. All were different colors and uniquely their own. Micky Muggles had left no footprint. I shook my head and waited for more. I didn't have to wait long.

Lura Belle took over. "I recognized the deranged egomaniac amidst all that dragon testicle nonsense. It's like the waste of humanity wrote it himself."

She definitely had our attention. Although, it was kind of a pot-kettle-black for her to call Micky Muggles a waste of humanity.

"Keep going," I said, feeling breathless and antsy.

Dimple rolled her eyes and pushed Lura Belle back down on the couch. "The only thing a Nephilim needs to extend their lives is magic. That bat-fowling, clack-dish imbecile developed a way to siphon the power from those who live for eternity."

"Of course, there are prices to pay from committing a crime so base," Jolly Sue said.

"Like what?" I asked.

"Complete and utter destruction of the mind," she answered. "It's a deadly and dangerous game to play. There's a reason greed is one of the Seven Deadly Sins."

"He's a dumb mother fucker for sure," Candy Vargo ground out. "Not a whole lot of cells in that fugly noggin."

"Can any of this be true?" I asked my posse of really old and Immortal friends.

Candy Vargo paced the room, deep in thought. Tim had leaned forward and dropped his head to his hands. Heather simply appeared confused. But Charlie... he was furious. His power roared to the surface and breathing became an optional sport. My mild-mannered friend was sparking and glowing so bright it was difficult to look at him.

"Can't breathe," I choked out.

He tamped back his power with effort. "More," he demanded of the Nephilim in a voice so terrifying, I almost hid.

The trio didn't blink an eye. It was shocking. Were they missing the fear gene? Their sense of self-preservation was nil.

"Take down the cage," Dimple snapped. "It's rude and unmannerly."

Charlie turned to Candy. "Take it down."

She didn't sass Charlie. Nobody ever talked back to the Immortal Enforcer. Candy was all business. With a wave of her hand, the bubble disintegrated. Pale peach sparkles floated through the air as the cage collapsed.

"What's in the hoard?" Lura Belle asked, brushing glitter off her peas. "Immortals?"

"Yes," I replied. "The Grim Reaper, the Archangel, two others… and Zadkiel."

Dimple's blue eyes grew stormy. "We were told he was dead."

"He is," I assured her. "It's his ghost."

"Can you see ghosts?" Heather asked.

"Don't know," Jolly Sue admitted.

I stared at the women. They stared back. The answer to Heather's question felt important. I had a way to get the answer.

"Here's the deal," I said flatly. "I'm going to call down a ghost. If you harm her, you're dead. If you say the words to the spell, you're dead. If you try to pull a fast one, you're dead. Am I clear?"

"Lovely manners," Jolly Sue said with a sour expression.

"Thank you," I replied evenly.

"That wasn't a compliment," she snapped.

"Yep. I know."

I walked over to the stairs and called up to Gram. Turning slowly, I faced the Nephilim as I waited.

The rules had changed. I knew in my gut they had changed for a reason. I just had no idea what the reason was. Finding out was a piece of the puzzle. Ignoring what was in front of me wasn't going to help. At this point, it was unclear if it was fate, the higher power or just dumb luck directing me.

Didn't matter. I was playing to win.

CHAPTER SIX

"LORDY HELP US ALL. IF IT AIN'T THE THREE STOOGES," GRAM
muttered under her breath as she floated down the stairs.
She eyed the Nephilim with distrust. Gram had known the
women forever and a day. There had never been any love
lost.

Dimple, Jolly Sue and Lura Belle sat on the couch and
picked at their food. Their gazes were aimed in the direction of Gram, but their faces held no expression. I couldn't
tell if they could see her or not.

Behind Gram were Prue, Rafe, Abby and Mr. Johnson.
The sweet old ghost was suspended in the air and hiding
behind Rafe. Dirk—now back to his normal self—stood at
the top of the stairs and eyed the scene below. Thankfully,
his horse wasn't with him. For a hot sec I wondered if the
horse was in my bedroom, but decided not to give it too
much thought. My house was already a mess, if there was a
horse in my bedroom hanging out with my dogs, so be it.

"Well now," Gram said, hovering at my side with raised brows and a chuckle. "Y'all are looking like ten miles of bad road. Guess bein' mean as snakes has finally caught up with you."

"Take that back, old woman," Dimple snapped, looking like she'd seen a ghost... because she had.

"One question answered," I said. I wasn't sure why I wanted to know if the Nephilim could see the ghosts, but it felt necessary. I wasn't going against my gut for any reason. Doing that in the past had bitten me in the butt.

Now that I knew, we needed to move on quickly. They didn't get the memo.

Jolly Sue jumped right on in. She wagged her finger at Gram. "You're so fulla crap your eyes are brown!"

Lura Belle—or Lura Hell as I'd secretly named her—was not one to be left out. "You look so crappy, I'd hire you to haunt a house."

Gram grinned. "Beware of what you wish for, Lura Belle."

"Burn," Candy Vargo said, giving Gram a thumbs up.

"Paaaalease," Dimple snapped with an eye roll as she sneered at Gram. "You couldn't haunt a house. You're so daft, you haven't got the sense the good Lord gave a goose."

"Weak," Candy commented, clearly keeping score.

Dimple hissed at Candy Vargo.

Candy laughed.

Shit was going south.

"Maybe I ain't got no sense," Gram agreed, zipping back and forth in front of the nasty trio. "But I heard that there's a tree stump in Louisiana with a higher IQ than you."

All three Nephilim gasped and glared. With their eyes narrowed dangerously they looked like vipers. Everyone in the room watched the showdown. When I felt Tory squeeze my arm, I almost jumped out of my skin.

"You can show yourself," I whispered softly.

"Not yet," she whispered in my ear.

"I'm gonna give that comeback a ten," Candy announced. "Gram's winnin'."

"That dead woman is *not* winning," Jolly Sue shouted, jumping to her feet. "She was so ugly when she was born her mamma used to borrow a baby to take to church on Sunday."

The Keeper of Fate glanced over at Gram. "That one was pretty good."

Gram shrugged and rubbed her papery hands together with glee. She did a few ungraceful flips in the air then hovered right in front of Jolly Sue. "If I had a dog as ugly as you, I'd shave his butt and make him walk backwards."

Dimple laughed. Jolly Sue slapped her. Lura Belle growled at them, and they both backhanded Lura Belle.

Shit had gone south then taken a U-turn into Crazy Town. I glanced back and forth between my usually polite Gram and Candy Vargo. All the time while Gram was teaching The Keeper of Fate to be courteous, it looked like Fate had also been giving lessons. I'd never heard Gram throw so many insults. It was nuts.

Candy Vargo snapped her fingers and conjured up a big bowl of popcorn. She made herself comfortable and watched the bizarre roast unfold.

Lura Belle's mouth hung open in a state of shock at

being smacked. Furious was a mild word to use for her
reaction. Instead of retaliating with a right hook, she went
for the jugular. "Dimple and Jolly Sue, your lips look like a
prolapsed baboon anus."

Candy Vargo fell to the floor in laughter, throwing her
snack bowl in the air. There was popcorn everywhere.
Whatever. I was sure there was horse poop in my
bedroom.

"Prolapsed baboon anus!" Candy slapped her knee.
"Good one," she egged them on. "That was a sure-fire ten!"

I bit back a laugh. It was difficult to believe I could laugh
while my world was imploding, but funny was funny.
Prolapsed baboon anus was far more descriptive and accurate than cat-butt face.

Dimple came back first. She went nose to nose with
Lura Belle. "I can get a nip and a tuck for my short comings,
you bawdy, crook-plated hussy. You, on the other hand, will
be stupid for eternity."

"Darn tootin'," Jolly Sue grunted. "Oh, Lura Belle, don't
stand too close to the fire… plastic melts."

"Enough," I ground out. This was ridiculous and a
distraction I didn't need. Lives were at stake, lives of people
I loved, and we were watching old ladies hurl offensive
putdowns at each other. They'd read the shorthand. I'd
figure out how to repay them at another time. "While I'll
admit the insults are professional level, that's not why we've
gathered. In fact, I think Lura Belle, Dimple and Jolly Sue
should leave."

Tory who'd been invisible, reversed the magic and joined
us in her solid body. She stared at me for a long beat then

shook her head. I squinted at her for more of an explanation. She simply shook her head again.

"Umm… okay… I've changed my mind," I announced, unclear as to why. "I'd like the Nephilim to stay, please."

Gram shot around the room like a bird on crack. The old ladies observed her warily. Mr. Jackson cheered and clapped.

"Plaaayah gaaameah?" Mr. Jackson asked, turning a flip and losing his foot.

I picked it up and put it on the coffee table. Reattaching it would have to wait. The Nephilim recoiled. Lura Belle, Dimple and Jolly Sue stared in horror at Mr. Jackson.

"Oh my God," Dimple shrieked. "What is that?"

"What's wrong with him?" Jolly Sue demanded, pointing at Mr. Jackson. "He's hideous. Where's the rest of his head, for the love of everything revolting?"

"Get thee away, disgusting entity!" Lura Belle crossed her fingers at him before grabbing a pillow from my couch and tossing it at the old man.

It went right through him. However, the intent was obvious. Mr. Jackson trembled and looked like he was going to cry.

I was so done. Insult me. Fine. Insult my dead friends. That's a big nope.

Scarily, Gram was more done than I was.

"No way, no how," Gram bellowed, shocking all with her red-hot anger. "I have a right mind to cancel your birth certificates."

The Nephilim fell back onto the couch and cowered. Even Candy Vargo's eyes grew wide. Considering she was usually on the end of Gram's tirades, it was surprising. However, there was a big difference. Gram got on Candy's butt because she loved her. Gram didn't love Dimple, Jolly Sue or Lura Belle.

Gram kept going in a voice so loud, it echoed through the huge house and bounced off the walls. "Lemme tell you vile old geezers somethin'. Mr. Jackson is a better person than any of you three could dream of bein'."

She was so agitated she flew right through me. The rush of icy pain was intense. I didn't say a word or even flinch.

"Mr. Jackson," Gram continued. "Mr. Harold Jackson is a hero. That man is missin' half his head because he saved his daughter and grandbabies from a fire. A beam fell from the ceiling and cracked his noggin. But you wanna know what? That man, with half a dang noggin, still got two babies and his daughter to safety before he bit it. DO YOU HEAR ME? Mr. Harold Jackson died givin' his life for people he loved. Don't you ever speak of the dead in such a disrespectful manner again. Ain't nobody loves any of you piss-ants enough to piss on you if you were on fire, let alone give their life to save you. Mr. Jackson is the best kind of human... and you're the worst."

The old ladies were speechless. I was also speechless and heartbroken for Mr. Jackson. It was easy to fall in love with the sweet ghost. His story was beautifully tragic. As soon as we saved Gideon and the others, Mr. Harold Jackson was on the top of my list to help.

And we *would* save Gideon and the others. The alternative wasn't acceptable.

Of course, Gram had more to say. My beloved grandmother always had more to say. "Y'all ain't never been nothin' but trash," she accused the women. "You never had a kind word or did nothin' nice for a single soul. People are gonna dance on your graves when you die. And I'll be dancin' with 'em."

"Not our fault," Dimple whimpered, looking defeated.

"Bull-honkey," Gram spat. "You had choices. You blew 'em. Every dang day of your miserable lives you blew 'em. All three of you mean-ass cowards deserve whatever's comin' for you."

"Well motherfuckin' shit monsters," Candy said with a huge groan. She walked in a tight circle and punched herself in the head. Twice. "As much as it pains me—and it *really* fuckin' pains me, that asshole Dimple is tellin' the truth."

"What, Candy girl?" Gram asked, confused.

"Tim, can you take it from here?" Candy begged. "If I have to defend those prolapsed baboon anuses, I might do somethin' I'll regret."

"Your maturity is to be commended, friend," Tim told Candy with a smile. "And yes, I'll take the lead on this one. I skipped breakfast, so there's less of a chance of projectile vomiting."

I held up my hands and shook my head. "No. There isn't time for this. We have the spell. We need to get to the hoard. Sundown is only a few hours away."

Tory placed her hand on my cheek. "When something is in front of you, deal with it. If you don't, it will deal with you and the results will not be pretty."

Her words were a gut punch—one I needed. Charlie compounded it with a metaphorical left jab.

"I don't understand why dissecting the Nephilim is pertinent, but in my thousands of years I've discovered little is left up to chance," he said. "The Immortal world gives to those who have their eyes wide open and takes from those whose eyes are closed. Keep your eyes open, Daisy."

My chin dropped to my chest, and I tried to beat back the panic that was doing its best to consume me. "I'm wrong. You're right. Thank you."

Heather walked over, took my hand in hers and squeezed. "Nothing is impossible, you just have to believe. Every moment counts. Use all of them wisely."

I smiled at my sister. "I will." Turning to Tim, I nodded. "Please continue, friend."

"With pleasure," he replied. "So Gram, as Candy was saying, Dimple, Jolly Sue and Lura Belle come by their hideousness by the nature of their birthright."

Gram scratched her head in confusion. "Timmy boy, I'm not followin' that. You're gonna need to speak plain English."

"My apologies," he said. "The ladies are not fully human. They're the product of an Angel mating with a human. They're Nephilim."

"Like Daisy?" Gram questioned.

"Nothing like Daisy," Heather said. "Dimple, Jolly Sue and Lura Belle aren't Immortal. They have powers, but they don't live forever."

"Thank God for that," Gram muttered. "But now, I thought most Angels were the good guys."

I laughed without an ounce of humor in it. "Some are.

Some aren't. The Angel in question is Zadkiel. Zadkiel is their father."

All three of the Nephilim growled. They were joined by Prue, Rafe, Abby and Tory. It sounded like a pack of wild animals in my living room.

"Well slap my ass and call me Sally," Gram shouted. "Now it makes sense. Didn't think it was possible for people to be as mean as them three, but I stand corrected. Zadkiel is a real sumbitch."

The three women looked far older than their advanced years. Every wrinkle was pronounced, their cornflower blue eyes were dull and their skin appeared grayish.

Dimple stood up. She was no longer sneering or gloating. "We had gifts bestowed upon us by the monster who sired us," she said in a flat and lifeless tone. "Mine is to create bad luck. It's innate. I can't control it."

Jolly Sue stood up next to her sister. Her face was twisted in embarrassment and shame. "Mine is to make someone act on their worst impulses."

Lura Sue just sat there with her arms crossed over her chest and pouted.

"Don't make me slap you into next week. Because I will," Dimple warned.

The holdout stood up. She was half the woman she'd appeared to be only moments ago. "My gift—for lack of a better word—is to make people see the worst in themselves."

I needed to have my head examined. I felt sorry for all three of them.

"Holy Hell," Gram said, shaking her head. "Can't you give them gifts back?"

Jolly Sue sighed. "We've tried."

"Each time we tried… and we've tried many times, they come back tenfold," Dimple whispered.

"That motherfucker needs to DIE," Candy Vargo shouted, walking over to the wall and punching both fists through it.

"He's already dead," Tory reminded her.

"Right, my bad," Candy conceded, picking up a lamp and smashing it into the TV. "Oh, and just a heads up to those fuckers who missed it. Micky Fuckin' Muggles is a Nephilim. Not Immortal. The pains in the ass on the couch clued us in."

I was going to need a new house when all was said and done.

"Impossible," Abby said.

"Nope. It's very possible," I replied.

Prue, Rafe and Abby approached the Nephilim. My siblings' eyes were glowing a bright gold and their downy white wings burst from their backs. They were a sight to behold. The trio of old women shrunk back in fear.

"Tell us what you found in the shorthand," Rafe demanded.

Charlie clapped his hands and brought back Agnes' notes. I wasn't sure where he'd sent them, but was glad to see them again. He handed them to Jolly Sue. She quickly rifled through the pages and pulled out a single sheet. Her hands shook.

She looked up at me for approval. I nodded.

Jolly Sue recited the spell passage again. "To find the plane, one must break the chain. It must be broken by one of their own. The words have magic. They must be used before all becomes tragic. The key is to destroy the *catabibazon* to stop other hoards. In that place the enchantment is stored." She swallowed loudly then continued. "All good things come in three. If you plant the seed, it becomes a tree. To find the dragon, say the words. But be very careful when the worlds grow blurred… Draca. Dreki. Draco."

Again, the house trembled on its foundation.

"Hells bells," Candy shouted. "Do NOT say that spell again. The third time might be the charm, and we ain't got no fuckin' plan yet."

"He isn't Beetlejuice or Bloody Mary," Heather said.

"Nope," Charlie agreed. "He's worse. He's a Nephilim who's figured out a way to harness Immortal magic."

Abby shuddered and glanced at Prue and Rafe. They took her hands. "Do we truly believe that Micky Muggles is a Nephilim?"

"It's a good question, but I'm leaning hard into yes," I said. "The gals said they recognized him from the notes. Said it sounded like he wrote it—which we know for a fact that he did help write it."

"Correct," Heather said then looked at the Nephilim. "Stop me if I'm wrong, but you all can confirm he's figured out a way to siphon magic from Immortals to elongate his life and increase his powers?"

"Yes," Lura Belle said tightly. "He bragged about it one time when he was drunk at Sweet-pea's Bar and Grill about twenty years back. Everyone thought he was just making up a tall tale. We knew differently."

"Did he say how he did it?" Tim questioned. "As far as I knew, magic can be given willingly, but not stolen."

"He only said he did it," Lura Belle said. "Not how he did it."

Rafe's forehead creased. "He's been alive for at least several thousand years. Is that really possible if he's a Nephilim—even with stealing the magic?"

"Unfortunately, yes," Charlie said. "It makes sense. We have a registry of all the Immortals living on this plane—or most of them. While an Immortal can live forever, he or she can also die. Generally, we're aware when someone dies. However, there are upwards of five hundred missing persons cases over the last few thousand years."

"Also, does anyone find it odd when Zander beat the hell out of Micky that he didn't heal?" I asked.

"Interesting," Tim said, taking notes on his laptop. "There's a fine chance he used up whatever power he had to drop the barrier that kept you and Zander on the inside with him and all of us on the outside. Hence, not being able to magically heal is another check in the Nephilim column."

Prue sat down next to the old gals. It was clear that they were dying to touch her wings. She smiled at them and nodded. All three old women reached out and reverently stroked the shimmering feathers. Dimple began to weep. Jolly Sue swiped at her own tears. Lura Belle didn't have much emotion, but her mouth trembled and gave her away.

Prue pointed at me and spoke. "If we're to believe that

Agnes' fiction is indeed truth, then the directions have to be heeded."

"I agree," I said.

She raised a brow. "Do you?"

"Not following," I said, then pinned her with a stare. "No cryptic bullshit. Get straight to the point."

"Bullcrap, Daisy girl," Gram corrected me.

"Sorry," I said. "I meant, no cryptic bullcrap."

"Much better," Gram said, patting my head.

I might be a forty-year-old woman who happened to be the Death Counselor, the Angel of Mercy and a brand-new mother, but I would always be Gram's little girl.

Prue winked at me. I winked back. Gram was a piece of work and we all loved her.

"We need to dissect the directions to understand them," she said.

"Good thinking," Abby agreed.

Both she and Rafe had joined the women on the couch. I sucked in an audible breath as I stared at them. Part of the directions stated that all good things came in three. There were three full Angels and three full Nephilim in my home. I didn't count. I was more of a freak of nature. Charlie was right. This was happening for a reason.

Now to figure out what that was. "Let's decipher the directions."

"And then go kick some ass," Candy Vargo added.

I couldn't have agreed more. The clock was ticking, but we had the beginnings of a plan. All we had to do was firm it up.

CHAPTER SEVEN

MY STRESS WAS SO HIGH, I GRABBED ONE OF THE BISCUITS
and ate it. It was still warm and tasted delicious. They were
for the guests, but Tim had made plenty. I wasn't going to
touch the creamed peas. The combo was gross and unappe-
tizing. The Nephilim and the Angels stayed seated together
on the couch. Gram and Mr. Jackson floated high in the air
by the chandelier. Tim was in the overstuffed chair and
Heather sat on the arm. Tory stood next to me while both
Candy and Charlie paced. Dirk was still at the top of the
stairs.

"To find the plane, one must break the chain," Tim read
aloud.

"Easy," Candy Vargo said, opening a new box of toothpicks and popping a few into her mouth. "Means to enter
the parallel plane you need the spell."

"Agreed," Charlie said. "The next line concerns me—It

must be broken by one of their own," he said, looking over Tim's shoulder and reciting the line.

"My guess is that means a Nephilim is needed to chant the spell," Dimple said. Her sisters nodded in agreement.

Everything was so insane. I had a feeling she might be correct. The fact that we'd only brought them in to read the shorthand on Gram's suggestion was nuts, further proving that very little in the Immortal realm was left to chance. Ironically, it appeared they were a piece of the puzzle that we needed.

"The house did rumble when they said the three words of the spell," Heather pointed out.

We all mulled the strange twist in silence. Only Tory was nonplussed. She'd been the one to insist the Nephilim stay. It took an army…

"I'm not convinced of that, but if it's accurate precautions must be taken," Rafe said in a strained tone.

"Like what?" I asked.

He looked at the trio of old women and sighed. "We'll get to that shortly. Let's stick to the directions. One step at a time."

"Next part is logical," Tim said, studying the computer screen. "The words have magic. They must be used before all becomes tragic." He looked up at everyone. "Basically, chant the spell and save the day."

If it were only that easy. The unknown was terrifying. That wouldn't stop me, but it was unnerving. I pictured Gideon and Alana Catherine's faces in my mind and my resolve grew stronger. The magic pumping through my veins made me feel a little light headed, but that was fine. I had the power to complete the mission. I just needed the plan to do it right.

Heather leaned in and looked at the screen. "It's the next line that's confusing—The key is to destroy the *catabibazon* to stop other hoards. In that place, the enchantment is stored." She threw up her hands in defeat. "I don't know what any of this means."

"Join the club," I said. Going through the instructions, line by line, wasn't making it much clearer. "Does anyone understand this cryptic mumbo-jumbo?"

"Iiiiah doooooooah!" Mr. Jackson said, flying over to Heather and hovering in front of her. He quivered spastically with excitement and lost a leg.

To everyone's great surprise, Lura Belle jumped up and tried to pick it up and hand it back to him. The gesture was one of kindness. Even the Nephilim seemed shocked by her action. As expected, her hand went right through the leg, but it was the unselfish thought that counted.

"I've got it. Thank you," I told her, gently patting her back.

She was startled by my kind touch and scurried back to the couch. I picked up the leg and added it to the growing pile of body parts on the coffee table. Turning back to Mr. Jackson, I smiled. "Can you tell us what it means?" I hoped we wouldn't have to endure knock-knock jokes to get the answer, but I was all in if that was the way he wanted to play.

"Yeeeeesah," he said with a giggle. "Meeeeeansah theeeeah dragooonsss taailah!"

"Holy shit," Candy shouted, giving Mr. Jackson a thumbs

up. "Our old boy is correct. I shoulda recognized that from reading all of Agnes' books. In astrology it means the moon's descending node—the dragon's tail."

I stared at Charlie. "That would've been a better definition."

He quirked his brow as he met my gaze. "I know what I know." He gestured to Candy. "She knows what she knows. We're not omnipotent."

I nodded, ran my hands through my unruly curls and closed my eyes, then immediately opened them. Charlie's earlier warning was at the forefront in my mind.

I had to go into this situation eyes-wide-open. "One big problem. Micky Muggles isn't really a dragon. They don't exist."

"Are you certain?" Prue inquired.

I thought I was. "Your point?" I asked, unwilling to play any games other than knock-knock right now.

"The mind is a strange and mystical thing," she said. "If the price for the crimes Micky Muggles has committed over and over is complete destruction of the mind, what's to say he doesn't actually believe he is a dragon?"

Belief wasn't fact. "If we're going to debate what-ifs and fairytales, I'm going to scream."

"Here me out," Prue said.

I forced myself to play along. "Okay. Let's say he does believe he's a dragon. How does that help us?"

She raised a brow and tilted her head. Even though she was new to this plane after having been Zadkiel's slave along with Rafe, Abby and Gabe for thousands of years, I was reminded how old my sister truly was. Discounting anything she added was foolish.

"If he's lost his sanity and believes himself to be a dragon, he would follow the rules of the dragons," she said. "We have a blueprint with the notes and the books."

"As written by Agnes?" I asked.

"As written by Agnes," she confirmed.

I sucked my bottom lip into my mouth and let her theory sink in. "So then he stores the magic he steals in his tail?"

Candy Vargo grunted with laughter. "His ass. The imbecile stores the magic in his motherfuckin' ass."

There was a moment of loaded silence as everyone did their best not to laugh.

Everyone failed.

The absurdity of it all was too much. I laughed so hard tears streamed down my cheeks. It was wildly inappropriate, like laughing at a funeral, but it was cathartic. Even Dimple, Jolly Sue and Lura Belle laughed. It transformed them. My compassion was going to get the best of me where they were concerned. Yes, they were awful, but considering the circumstances, it wasn't their fault.

"When you find that redneck jackhole, just lop his dang ass off," Candy said. "He's a Nephilim—if you do it when he's low on power, it won't grow back."

I squinted at her. "Are you serious?"

"As a fuckin' heart attack," she replied.

Tim scratched his head. "Honestly, it might work, friend. It won't solve the problem of the hoard he's already created, but it will keep him from creating more."

"I can't believe I'm going to say this, but..." Heather began with a wince. "Candy is making sense."

"That kills you, don't it?" Candy Vargo inquired with a cackle.

"Totally dead," Heather replied evenly with a smile pulling at the corners of her lips. "But if the dragon can no longer store magic, he's impotent, so to speak."

"No longer able to siphon magic without somewhere to put it," Abby added. "No longer Immortal."

It was the weirdest thing I'd heard and I'd heard a lot of weird since I started seeing the dead. However, as unconventional as the method was, I wouldn't discount it. Batshit crazy had become my new modus operandi.

"Let's continue," Tim suggested, still unable to suppress his grin. "The next lines are—All good things come in three. If you plant the seed, it becomes a tree."

"And that's where I believe it gets complicated," Rafe said.

"Talk," I told him.

He nodded and stood. "I think the three are Dimple, Jolly Sue and Lura Belle." He sighed and pressed the bridge of his nose. "I believe to succeed—to grow the tree—they have to accompany you to the parallel plane to get the hoard."

Charlie didn't like that. "They won't survive it."

"Not necessarily," Rafe told him.

Charlie wanted Rafe to say more, but Dimple jumped in with her own two cents on the matter.

"Don't care," Dimple insisted, getting to her feet. "In my life, I've done nothing good. Nothing. And not by my own choice. If I can stop the imbalance I might not end up in the Darkness. I'll take that chance."

"Yep," Jolly Sue said, joining her sister. "I'm sick and tired of being the gleeting, venomed, goatish bitch that everyone hates. Dyin' would be a dang relief. I'm already a hundred and fifty years old. Not sure how much more time I have, but it can't be much. I'd like to go out a hero like Mr. Jackson."

Lura Belle stood up next and slapped both of her sisters. They slapped her back. Hard. She huffed and puffed for a moment then sighed so dramatically she looked deflated, as if she was a balloon running out of air. "I agree with my droning, lumpish, hugger-mugger sisters," she finally said. "I'd prefer to go out for a good cause."

"Why'd you punch 'em?" Gram asked.

Lura Belle shrugged. "It's fun."

Candy Vargo chuckled. "Can't say I disagree with that. I'd love to slap the shit out of all three of you."

"But you won't," I warned her.

The Keeper of Fate hemmed and hawed until Gram got up in her face and let her have it. It was a relief. I didn't want to have to electrocute Candy. She'd be pissed. A pissed Candy Vargo was a bad thing.

"I'll tell you what, little missy," Gram shouted, floating only inches from Candy's face. "I'm sick and tired of your rude behavior. If you keep it up, I'm gonna tie your tail in a knot, jerk you bald and cream your corn. You hear me?"

"Yes, ma'am," she replied contritely.

"Well now, that's good, sugar puff," Gram told her with a smile. "I love you too dang much to let you act like a hooligan. Them nasty women are trying to do some good to make up for all the shitty. Give 'em a chance before you wallop 'em."

It was beyond clear that the only person in the Universe that Candy would obey was the ghost who loved her like a daughter.

"I won't slap the shit out of Dimple, Jolly Sue or Lura Belle," Candy said, looking over at Gram for approval.

Gram blew her a kiss and the potential smackdown was averted.

"Rafe," I said, getting back on track. "Explain more, please."

He nodded. "Numbers are fascinating things. There are three Nephilim here and three full Angels."

Prue and Abby caught on immediately. I didn't. Neither did anyone else present.

"And?" I pressed.

"Power—or magic to be more specific—can be given willingly," Prue said with a smile to Rafe. "If stolen, it will destroy the thief."

"If given freely," Abby said, joining in. "It's simply a gift to be used until it runs out. It harms neither the giver or the taker."

I'd been given dark magic by the Demon Abaddon to help me defeat Zadkiel. It had been alarming, but necessary, and I'd been both honored and grateful. I was told it would eventually fade, but I could still feel it in my blood in times of dire circumstances. However, the power that my siblings would give to the three Nephilim would come from the Light...

"Wait," I said, pressing my temples. "Not sure I understand. If you were to gift the Nephilim power, would it increase the evil gifts they already have?"

"Excellent fuckin' question," Candy Vargo said, offering me a toothpick.

I took it and put it in my mouth. I avoided eye contact with Gram. She wasn't fond of people chewing on toothpicks. I wasn't either, but they seemed to help me focus. Between chomping on wood and pinching my weenus, I was full of homemade remedies.

"Yes and no," Rafe said. "The good would overwhelm the bad, but they would still be able to cause bad luck, make someone act on their worst impulses and lead a person to see the worst in herself or himself. However, it would give them more protection as well."

I pursed my lips in thought. Worries and questions raced through my mind. All of them were important and I couldn't figure out which one to ask first. Heather lent a hand.

"Okay," she said in her lawyer voice. "With an increase in magic, would the Nephilim be able to use the powers on Immortals?"

Abby, Prue and Rafe exchanged perplexed glances. That wasn't the reaction I was looking for.

"My guess would be no, but we'd have to test it after the exchange is done," Abby answered.

"You know," Tim said, steepling his hands and tapping his fingers together. "If the powers they have are increased, they could be used against Micky Muggles. He's a Nephilim."

"Nothing would give me more pleasure," Jolly Sue announced. "I don't like that slimy lewdster one bit."

"Question is," Candy Vargo said, walking over the trio of old gals. "Are you ready to remove an ass?"

Dimple's face screwed up in disgust. "Literally or figuratively?"

"Literally," Candy challenged.

"Yes," Lura Belle snapped. "I'll bite the currish, mangled, reeky nut-hook's ass off if necessary. *Literally.*" She punctuated her statement by baring her teeth.

"Holy shit," Candy said, bowing to Lura Belle. "My kind of bitchy badass."

Lura Belle blushed a deep red. She was over the moon. It was probably the first time in her life someone had given her a compliment. Granted, it was about cannibalism, but a compliment was a compliment no matter how off color.

My thoughts were all over the place. I began to pace the room. I was fully aware I was sparking like a bomb about to detonate.

"Talk it out, Daisy," Tim suggested. "Let us help you make sense of the turmoil in your head."

I smiled at my friend and stopped pacing. Inhaling deeply then blowing it out slowly, I pinched my weenus and felt centered enough to let it rip. "Is it insane to think that the gals could distract Micky Muggles with their gifts while I get Gideon, Gabe and the others to safety?"

"Everything we do is insane," Tory pointed out.

I stared at her for a long beat then made another decision. "I want you with me, and I want you invisible." My request was twofold. Her power was incredible. That was a big plus. However, it was her love for Gabe—that she kept denying—that would make her invaluable by my side.

She nodded and smiled. "I would be honored."

"One of my worries, among a shitload, is that Dimple, Jolly Sue and Lura Belle could be harmed in a permanent way... even with the exchange of magic," I said.

"We don't care," Dimple reminded me.

"But I do," I shot back.

"Listen fuckers," Candy Vargo told them. "You're dealin' with the Angel of Mercy. Now, I wouldn't give a rat's ass about you bitin' it, but Daisy's a different breed of Immortal. She's *nice*."

I rolled my eyes. There were lots of people who wouldn't describe me as nice—Zadkiel was one of them. "Actually, you're *nice* too, Candy Vargo—mother of a bunch of sweet foster children."

"Fuck you," she said, giving me the middle finger salute and a wide smile.

"Right back at you," I replied. I threw my question back in the ring. "Would the gals be safe?"

"Safety is never a guarantee," Prue said. "Our world is violent."

"Understatement," I muttered.

"But," Tory chimed in. "If no one can see me, I can cover the Nephilim while you work to get the prisoners free."

"If they're still alive," Candy said.

"Nope," I snapped, slashing my hand through the air and throwing a zap of white-hot energy at her. "Don't even say that. Don't even think it."

Instead of retaliating, my nutty friend saluted me. "Roger that, fucker."

"All of this is risky," Charlie said, staring directly at the Nephilim. "Trusting them could be a mistake—a mistake that could be the beginning of the end."

The Horseman known as Death bellowed down from his spot at the top of the stairs. "The one who giveth can taketh away. Or if denied, the next one can."

My eyes grew huge as the meaning hit me like a Mack truck. Charlie's concern was spot on. Being careless with Gideon and the other's lives wasn't on the table. But if I needed the Nephilim to get to the hoard, it was imperative that we knew they wouldn't turn on us. Their track records weren't stellar.

Dirk might have just given me a clue to the reassurance we all needed. Candy's ass message for the win… maybe.

"From your mouth…" I whispered. Sprinting over to the bottom of the stairs, I looked up at Dirk. The gorgeous drag queen winked. "You have your bargaining chip now, darling. Use it. The ass don't lie."

I turned back to the Nephilim. "Tell me your fondest wish." I held my breath and crossed my fingers. If it wasn't what I thought it was, I didn't have a bargaining chip. "Not something you think I want to hear. Tell me the truth."

Dimple raised her hand and stood up. "I don't wanna be a psychotic bitch anymore," she choked out then held up her hands to her face just in case one of her sisters punched her. "I don't want to be compelled to make people have bad luck. I'm weary… and tired of being despised."

I almost screamed with excitement, but there were two more to go. I held it back and kept my expression neutral.

Jolly Sue put her arm around her sister. Dimple flinched then leaned into Jolly Sue for comfort. The two women looked awkward and uncomfortable showing vulnerability, but it was sweet in a tragic way.

"If wishes were horses, beggars would ride," Jolly Sue mumbled. "I can't undo any of the dreadful deeds I've done, but I'd like to live out my twilight years not making people act on their worst impulses." She stared at the ground for a long beat, then sighed. "Full disclosure—I used to enjoy it. I don't anymore. Most of my waking thoughts are filled with the expressions of horror on my victims' faces, and my nightmares... I wouldn't wish on my worst enemy."

"And you have lots of those," Dimple said.

"True that," Jolly Sue agreed.

Lura Belle slapped both of her sisters. She then turned to Candy Vargo and held out her hand. "Give me a toothpick," she snapped.

Candy raised a brow then walked over to her and obliged. The sour faced Nephilim put it between her teeth. She chewed on it for a bit then wedged herself between her sisters. They warily let her in and leaned away. I didn't blame them. Lura Belle was fond of throwing punches.

"While eliminating the power of making people see the worst in themselves would be grand, what I want more is to make that bastard Zadkiel pay," she hissed.

"Get in line," Rafe said flatly.

"He thought it was a joke—we were a joke. He made us subhuman and defective. I've lived for a hundred and sixty years as a pariah," she ground out, angrily swiping tears from her wrinkled cheeks. "That pig would visit us and laugh as we wreaked havoc on those who couldn't defend themselves. If we complained, we were infused with higher levels of depravity. I know he's already dead, but I'd like to kick his ass."

"Trust me," Tory said with a smile that was so blood-thirsty, it made me back away. "I have plans for Zadkiel that pale in comparison to anything you could do. I'll get your vengeance for you along with the others who want their pound of flesh."

"Who exactly are you?" Lura Belle asked.

"Purgatory," she replied.

"Otherwise known as Zadkiel's worst fuckin' night-mare," Candy Vargo added.

All three Nephilim walked over to Tory and shook her hand. It was a surreal moment and one I wouldn't forget. However, the clock was ticking.

I glanced over at Charlie. "I have a way to guarantee they won't go rogue."

"By all means, let's hear it," he replied.

"Zadkile bestowed the gifts. He can take them back," I said.

The Nephilim gasped.

"You think that fucker is gonna do the right thing?" Candy Vargo asked with a skeptical look on her face.

"Most likely not," I replied calmly.

Charlie shook his head. "Not following how that's the collateral we need."

"Ah, but it is," I replied. I had everyone's attention now. I turned to the old gals. "The ass don't lie."

Candy Vargo laughed. "Badasssssss," she shouted.

"Again, not understanding," Charlie said.

"The one who giveth can taketh away. Or if denied, the next one can." I paused for dramatic effect. "I'm the next one. If the son of a bitch says no, I have every right as the Angel of Mercy to make his wrong a right. Period."

"You would do that for us?" Dimple asked in a shaky voice.

The other two were open mouthed and in shock. My gut told me that they would have helped without an incentive. However, Charlie was absolutely right. There was too much at stake to just go with my gut on this one.

I nodded. "I would, but that depends on the three of you. If you defy me or work against me in any way whatsoever, the deal is off. The chances of Zadkiel agreeing to take back the gifts are lower than low. I'm a done deal if you keep your word. I need you to prove to me that you want to be good."

The Nephilim got down on their knees and bowed to me. It made me wildly uncomfortable. I walked over and gently helped them back to their feet. It's time."

"For?" Lura Belle asked with quivering lips.

"For the exchange of magic."

The Angels smiled at the Nephilim. I was about to watch a miracle.

CHAPTER EIGHT

"Is there gonna be bloodshed?" Candy Vargo asked, looking hopeful.

I rolled my eyes and hoped not. The power exchange with Abaddon had included the slashing of our hands and the exchange of blood. I was Immortal. I healed quickly. The Nephilim were not Immortal.

"No bloodshed," Abby said as she, Prue and Rafe moved all the furniture in the large room over to the walls. Tory and I helped them. Tim sat on the couch with the nervous Nephilim, and Candy Vargo polished off the rest of the biscuits.

"I'm going to ward the house and the property. Nothing comes in, and nothing leaves unless we approve it," Charlie said, pulling on a coat. "Heather and Dirk, I need you to reinforce the perimeter."

"Smart," Heather replied, taking the jacket Tory offered.

"But of course, handsome," Dirk told Charlie. The

gorgeous drag queen snapped his fingers. He was now clad in a floor-length hot pink fur. He curtsied to the group and then giggled. "Not to worry, darlings. It's faux!"

Heather grinned, grabbed his hand and pulled him out of the front door.

"Daisy girl," Gram said, hovering in the air. "You want me and Mr. Jackson to stay or go?"

I looked to Prue for the answer. She pointed to the stairs. "Go," I told Gram, giving her a kiss on her semi-transparent cheek. "Keep an eye on our other dead guests, please."

"Rightyroo!" she said, then zipped across the room and landed on the couch next to Dimple. "Y'all have been so crappy over the years you could make a preacher cuss. But I'm right proud of all three of you today! Just dills my pickle that you're turnin' a new leaf and gettin' your dang noses out of the air. Used to worry me thinkin' y'alls sniffers were so high and mighty you might drown in a rainstorm."

"I'm sure lots of townsfolk are hopin' we drown," Jolly Sue commented dryly.

"Yeppers," Gram told her. "But you bet your bippy that I'm gonna crow from the rooftops that y'all are battin' for the good guys now. Whole town's gonna know y'all are new and improved."

Lura Belle glanced over at Gram with a smile that looked like she was grinding her teeth. At least she was trying. "May I make an observation?" the Nephilim inquired.

"Go right ahead," Gram told her.

"You're dead."

Gram slapped her skinny thigh and cackled. "Fine point. Well made. Not a problem. I'll have my girl, Candy, tell everyone."

Candy groaned, spit out half of a chewed-up biscuit and looked like she'd swallowed a bag of lemons. She was close to a meltdown. Orange sparks popped around her head, and she glowed a bright green. The crazy woman was a toddler who could take down a house with a tantrum. Gram shot her a sharp look. The Keeper of Fate reined it in and refrained from destroying my home. Gram's tough love could cause miracles.

"Reeeeaaadyah?" Mr. Jackson asked Gram as he did a few flips. Thankfully, he didn't lose any more body parts—not that there were many more to lose.

"I am, Mr. Jackson," Gram said, taking the old man's good hand in hers. "Pretty sure a *Family Feud* marathon is comin' on!"

On that last remark, the ghosts floated up the stairs, debating who was better looking—Richard Dawson or Bob Barker.

My stomach was in knots. The unknown made me want to hurl. I could solve that. I pinched my weenus and took a calming breath. "Can you explain what you're about to do?" I asked my Angel siblings.

"Of course," Prue said as her wings danced and shimmered around her. "It's not violent or painful. We've done it before, and there were no complaints. It's a simple transfer of our power through physical touch."

"Good to know," I said, feeling less wonky. "How can we help?"

"You can't," Rafe said. "Just take a seat and enjoy the show."

Candy, Tim, Tory and I sat down on one of the couches. Tim clasped his hands in his lap. His eyes sparkled with excitement.

"I've never witnessed this before," he whispered. "So thrilling!"

The three Angels approached the trio of Nephilim and extended their hands. Dimple grabbed Prue's with no hesitation. Jolly Sue latched onto Rafe like he was a lifeline. The only attitude thrown was from Lura Belle. She reached into her purse, removed a sanitary wipe and handed it to Abby. My sister laughed and cleaned her palms and fingers. Lura Belle inspected them and then joined the party.

"Persnickety old bag," Candy Vargo whispered, shaking her head.

They formed a triangle. Each Nephilim faced her Angel. The sense of anticipation was heavy. As my siblings began to chant in a musical and unrecognizable language, golden magic filled the room and made it look like a storybook come to life. This was different from Charlie's magic, where it was difficult to breathe. The power from the three Angels was gentle and warm—made me feel as if I was floating on water instead of sitting on a couch.

Rafe, Prue and Abby flicked their fingers and shimmering dust in every color of the rainbow joined the magic. The dust swirled like tiny little clouds and bounced off of every surface in the room. When the Angels wings fluttered the dust, there was a bright flash and silver sparkles rained down on us.

"This is like takin' fuckin' acid," Candy commented under her breath.

Tim caught some of the enchantment in his hand and marveled at it. "I'd have to disagree, friend. It's more like doing shrooms."

I glanced at both of them in surprise. "Shrooms?" I asked, squinting at him.

Tim giggled. "Let's just say Candy and I were active during the 1960s hippy movement. Quite enjoyable."

"Honestly, I don't remember most of it," Candy admitted with a chuckle. "But if Tim says we had fun, then we did."

When my friends made statements like that it hit me hard how much more living they'd done than me. Gideon was older than dirt. Even if we spent the rest of eternity talking through his past, there wouldn't be enough time. I'd have to be satisfied making our own memories together. Not that he wasn't an open book, but I knew much of his past had been tragic. I never pressed him.

Immortality could be a blessing or a curse... or both. I hadn't chosen to become Immortal. It had chosen me. Diving into the minds of the dead had done something to my DNA. At first, I was devastated. Now, I wouldn't have it any other way. The two loves of my life—Gideon and our daughter, Alana Catherine—would be with me forever.

Well, as long as I could get to the portal and free him before Micky Muggles drained him of his magic.

"Shit," I muttered under my breath. I'd gone from feeling true peace bathed in the magic of the Angels to wanting to peel my skin off.

"One step at a time, Daisy," Tim said, touching my hand.

"If you force or rearrange the order, it creates chaos. There's still time."

I nodded jerkily and tried to be present in the moment. It was hard, but doable.

One by one the Angels kissed the foreheads of the Nephilim. The three old ladies grew weak in the knees and slowly sunk to the floor. Rafe clapped his hands and a burst of magic flew from his fingertips almost blinding me. Out of self-preservation, I put my hands over my eyes. When I removed them, the Nephilim were laying on a bed of downy Angel feathers.

Rafe, Prue and Abby smiled and lay down beside them. No one spoke and no one moved. Thin tendrils of golden light left the Angels and disappeared into the Nephilim. The smiles on Dimple, Jolly Sue and even Lura Belle's faces were stunning.

It was quiet.

It was lovely.

And then it was done.

Carefully, the Angels helped the Nephilim back to their feet. Prue glanced over at us.

"That's it," she said.

"I was really hoping for some blood," Candy griped.

"You're shit out of luck there," Rafe told her as he guided the old gals back to the other couch. "Light magic is peaceful and merciful."

Candy Vargo shrugged. "What happened to no pain, no gain? I like that better."

Abby rolled her eyes. "Of course, you do."

The Angels and Candy had a gnarly past, and that was an understatement. It was something I tried to never think about because the logistics were stomach churning. Way before I'd been born, Zadkiel had ordered the Angels to go after Candy. They did. As the story goes, they removed her appendages and left her defenseless. However, one should never assume that the Keeper of Fate is helpless. Never. Since she couldn't fight back with her missing limbs, she did what she claims was the only option left to her... she ate them.

The science of how they were back and fully formed beings was too much to think about without losing my mind. I needed my mind, so I refused to dissect that shitshow.

Tim approached the trio of ladies. "How do you feel?"

"Pretty darn good," Dimple said, rolling her neck and cracking her knuckles. "In fact, I haven't felt this good in decades."

"Ditto," Jolly Sue agreed. "I feel tingly and quite nice."

"Manners," Lura Belle shouted as she smacked her sisters and sent them flying. "You didn't say thank you."

"Neither did you, you fly-bitten, moldwarp," Dimple shrieked as she sprinted at Lura Belle and tackled her.

Jolly, not wanting to be left out, dove on top of both and them and pummeled away.

"Holy shit," Candy Vargo shouted with a grunt of laughter.

Holy shit was right. The fight was like watching a train-wreck. It was impossible to look away. Their new power was evident. They fought like twenty-year-old body builders who were fond of steroids. Jaw-dropping was the best way to describe it.

"Nope," Tory shouted and waved her hands. Gallons of water from out of nowhere, doused the Nephilim. The old gals screamed as they got soaked in icy water. "You stop that right now. We're not each other's enemy. If you keep that crap up, you're going to regret it."

The Nephilim were turning a little blue from the temperature of the water. That wasn't surprising. My secret nickname for Tory was prophetically accurate. The Ice Queen had just gotten the job done.

Tory eyed the women. "You can't put out a fire with an empty bucket," she said flatly. "My bucket is filled with ice."

Tim waved his hands and conjured up three big fluffy bath towels. He handed them to the drenched gals. "Save that wrath for Micky Muggles."

"Right," Candy said, plopping down in the arm chair. "About that… when you're ready to leave, all who are entering the parallel plane need to be touching or you're gonna get your ass left behind. Also, when you get there, stay low."

"Why?" I asked.

"Cause in that particular plane, according to Agnes' book, there're lasers that will lop your dang head off. Fry you to a fuckin' crisp."

"I'm sorry, what?" I asked.

"Lasers, motherfucker," she repeated. "Placed about five feet up and pointed at the center of the room."

"Umm… have you been there?" Jolly Sue asked.

"Kinda," Candy told her. "I've read the book… about

forty times."

I stared at Candy Vargo and made another decision. I didn't think taking too many people was a great idea, but I'd be stupid to leave her behind. She hadn't been a first choice because of her out of control penchant for violence, but she knew Agnes' stories better than the woman had herself.

"Was the layout in the book the same as my house?" I asked.

Candy shook her head. "Nope. But if that mullet-headed shitball is using the story as a blueprint then I say we take fuckin' heed of what Agnes' Bubbala wrote."

"Brilliant!" Tim said. "Any other life or death situations Daisy needs to be aware of?"

"The hoard will be hidden in plain sight," she shared.

"Meaning?"

"Meaning it'll be in the room even if you can't see it."

"Okay, then how did the good dragons in the novel find the prisoners?" I asked, kind of shocked that I was talking about fiction as if it were real. But... if we were going on the assumption that Micky Muggles believed he was actually a dragon, I would be a fool not to learn as much as I could.

I might be many things, but I was not a fool.

Candy chuckled. "You ever look at one of those Magic Eye pictures that looks like a bunch of squiggles, but when you blur your eyes, a picture forms?"

"I do," I told her. "My dentist had one that if you squinted just right, you could see several dolphins jumping out of the water."

"Do that," she advised. "Squint and let your eyes blur until all that's murky becomes clear."

"Wild," Tory muttered.

"Candy, I want you to come with us," I said. "I need you."

She pulled the toothpick out of her mouth and grinned. "Wouldn't miss that shit for the world. I'm in."

"Perimeter is set. House and the acreage around it are secured," Charlie announced as he walked back into the house.

Heather and Dirk were right behind him. Their eyes were wide as they took in the scene. The living room was filled with feathers and glitter of every color ever created. It was a beautiful mess.

"Interesting," Charlie mused.

Heather shook her head. "It looks like a bunch of chickens got into a glitter fight."

Candy snickered.

Dirk pressed his fingers to his chest. "What a wonderful boa I could create with these gorgeous plumes!"

"Awesome." I shook my head. "The feathers are cool," I told them. "But it's time to go."

"Hang on, darling," Dirk said, scooping up a handful of sparkles and sprinkling them on his wig. "Who are you taking with you?"

"Tory, Dimple, Jolly Sue, Lura Belle, Candy Vargo and me," I said.

He pursed his lips as he considered my team. "Not good," he said. "If you're in an army of even numbers, it's a battle against the odds."

I narrowed my gaze at the fabulous Horseman of Death. "Not sure I get that."

Dirk stood in front of me and smiled. "No worries,

darling. That's why I'm here." He winked. "There are those who might negate my intelligence due to my arresting and legendary beauty." The queen popped his tongue and adjusted his falsies with a giggle. "Those people are *not* smart. You, sugar pants, are smart! Now then, some—like myself—might interpret the meaning as... if two opposing armies being of equal numbers meet, the outcome shall be iffy."

"Okay," I said, still confused. "It's not two armies fighting. It's us against Micky Muggles."

"Is it?" he inquired, raising his perfectly plucked brow.

"Umm... no?" I answered, thinking that was what he wanted to hear even though I had no clue as to why.

"Bingo! Micky Muggles has taken power from Gideon, Gabe, Zander, Catriona and Zadkiel. Add one stupid Nephilim with the magic of many to the mix and it's an army of six."

"Oh my God," I said, taking that in. My friends were brilliant, and I'd be lost without them. "What do you suggest?"

"Take one more with you. Make your number odd—in every sense of the word—and make the armies uneven, sweet cheeks!" Dirk said.

"Seven is a powerful number," Charlie commented.

"Oh yes!" Tim said. "Seven has much spiritual significance. It's believed to attract positive energy and good fortune. Along with that, in several religious traditions the number seven holds a plethora of symbolism—often associated with divine forces!"

"Yep," Candy Vargo chimed in. "And if Daisy had read

the fuckin' Bible, she'd know that it also means full and complete world."

"Enough with the razzing about not reading the Bible… yet," I said. "It's on the list."

"Most of the Bible is off," Tory commented. "Although, I agree with Tim, Charlie and Candy about the number seven. In the metaphysical philosophy of numerology, the number seven relates to the Greek deity, Athena, and the Roman, Minerva. They were both goddesses of war and both protectors of cities. If we go with the number seven, we have a better chance of being intuitive and wise."

I was convinced. It was just a matter of who to take.

"Prue," Tim said. "I believe the seventh soldier should be Prue."

"Reasoning?" I asked. I was leaning towards Dirk.

"Give me a moment," Tim said as he reached into the pocket of his mail uniform and pulled out a small shiny bluish and brown stone. The strange and wonderful man circled the room and passed by each occupant. He watched the stone with intense focus. He left Prue for last. As he approached the Angel, the stone began to glow and vibrate in his hand.

"Yes!" Tim said, doing an awkward little jig. "I was correct. Just needed to double check since so much is on the line."

"What is that?" I asked.

Tim held it out. "It's a Blue Tiger's Eye," he explained. "It's a powerful crystal that can be quite helpful when making important decisions. Its innate power is the ability to enhance someone's intuition."

"The mail boy is a smart motherfucker," Candy announced.

"Thank you, friend," he said. "Anyhoo, the reason I think Prue is the addition you need is because she can infuse power into those without."

"So can Rafe and so can Abby. Why Prue?" I glanced over at my sister. "No offense. I have no problem taking you. I just want to clarify."

Prue held up her hands. "None taken. I have the same questions."

The Immortal Courier blushed. "Umm... I did eeny, meeny, miny, moe in my head first."

"Dude," I said, pressing my temples and wondering if he gone and lost it in the last few minutes. "Seriously?"

"Quite," he replied. "Any one of the three Angels have the ability that's needed. I wasn't sure which to choose since are all qualified and honorable. So... I did eeny, meeny."

"Makes sense to me," Candy volunteered. "I've flipped a coin upon occasion. Let fate make the decision when I'm confused."

"Aren't you Fate?" Dimple asked.

"The Keeper of," Candy acknowledged. "But sometimes fate is gonna be what fate's gonna be."

"I've rolled dice to make decisions once or twice," Heather admitted.

"On important situations?" I asked, unable to believe this was the method to their madness.

"Very," Heather told me.

Charlie joined the crazy. "I've wished on stars for guidance. One time I made a call based on the kind of cookie June made. Yes, for peanut butter. No, for chocolate chip."

"Holy snickerdoodle," I muttered.

"That would've been a maybe," Charlie added.

I sat down on the couch and rested my head in my hands. I was so tired of fighting. It felt as if my life since learning my true legacy had been nothing but battle after battle. I missed my child. I missed Gideon. This was the first time that I'd have to face an enemy without him, and if I lost, I could lose him forever. I clenched my fists, banishing the horrifying thought from my brain. I wouldn't lose. It wasn't an option. But I needed something more than a coin toss to show me we were on the right path.

"*Daisy!*" Gideon called out.

I let out a slight gasp as I looked around. It sounded like he was right next to me. He wasn't. But hearing his voice was beautiful music to my ears.

"*Gideon? Is it really you?*" Communicating with him telepathically was our party trick. Right now, it was a lifeline. I knew it might not last long.

"*Yes, there isn't much time,*" he replied.

"It's Gideon," I told everyone as I shushed them with my hands. The room went eerily silent. I swallowed the panic rising in my throat as I said, "*I'm listening.*"

"*He's after you and Alana Catherine,*" he rasped. "*Both of you get to safety. Trust no one until he's dead.*"

"*Alana Catherine is safe, and I'm coming for you,*" I informed him, trying not to cry.

"*Too dangerous. None of us are going to make it. We can't last much longer.*"

"No," I ordered. *"If you die, I'll kill you."*

His laugh was fatigued, but it filled my soul. I lived for his laugh. *"Zadkiel has done his best, but it's not enough."*

"Wait. What?" Had the power drain made him delusional?

"He's given of himself to all of us—what's left of his magic. He's close to being dust."

That was very hard to believe, but what in my life wasn't?

"Listen to me," I said in a tone that dared the Grim Reaper to defy me. *"You will hang on. We're close to rescuing you and everyone else. Promise me you'll hang on until I get there."*

"I promise I'll try," he answered.

My heart pounded in my chest, and I felt faint. But I had one last question to get in before the lines of communication disappeared. *"Is Micky Muggles there?"*

"Yes," he replied as his voice started to fade away. *"I love you, Daisy. Now and until the end of time."*

"I love you too... until the end of time," I whispered even though I knew he couldn't hear me. I glanced up at the people I loved and the ones who I was beginning to love. "They don't have much time left."

"Then it's time to fuckin' party," Candy Vargo ground out, gathering the group in the middle of the room. "Everyone, hold hands and don't let go. If you do, I have no fuckin' idea where you'll end up. Am I clear, fuckers?"

"You are, you boil-brained, rank, ratsbane," Lura Belle answered with a thumbs up.

"The spell has already been spoken twice," Tim reminded everyone. "It only needs to be said one last time."

"Everyone not going on the trip needs to leave the

room," Charlie advised.

"Roger that, darling," Dirk said, giving his arm to Heather and marching up the stairs. Rafe and Abby followed. Tim and Charlie brought up the rear.

"Take care, friends. Nothing is impossible as long as you believe," Tim said over his shoulder before he disappeared around the corner of the upstairs landing.

We said that often. It had become my mantra. I did believe. I believed with every fiber of my being. Failure was not an option.

"Ready" I asked.

Everyone nodded.

I held Tory and Candy's hands as I spoke. "Draca. Dreki. Draco."

Nothing happened. I almost puked.

"I've got this," Jolly Sue announced with so much pride she looked as if she might burst. "The spell was cast by a Nephilim. It shall be broken by a Nephilim."

Gratitude rushed through me. "Thank you, Jolly Sue." I prayed her solution worked.

She smiled and concentrated. "Draca. Dreki. Draco."

The living room shimmered and went fuzzy. It was working! Without warning, the Keeper of Fate gripped my hand so hard it made my bones crack. And then a scream parted my lips as my blood turned to acid in my veins and everything went black.

If I'd thought falling into the Darkness with the dead was intense, it had been nothing compared to getting sucked through a vortex into a parallel plane.

No pain. No gain.

CHAPTER NINE

My body felt as if it had been flattened by a steam roller then shoved through a shredder. The terror that shot through me shut down my lungs and refused to let me breathe. If we'd come this far only to be seared alive or suffocated, it would be devastating.

Candy and Tory had been on either side of me. I tried to reach out to them in the transport, but my limbs were useless.

The blood in my veins still burned like liquid fire.

My head pounded so intensely I was sure I'd burst an aneurysm. If this was the sensation one felt when entering a parallel plane due to Agnes' description in her book, she was a sadist. It sucked.

The excruciating pain ended in an explosion of snow-white crystals as we landed right back where we'd started. The relief was profound. Glancing around, I gasped. The room was entirely empty—not a single area rug, knickknack, or stick of furniture. The only things that hadn't disappeared was our motley crew of seven.

Candy Vargo's hair stood on end, and mine was floating around my head. It looked and felt as if we'd been electrocuted while being dipped in Hellfire. The Nephilim were shellshocked, but alive. Prue was definitely worse for the wear. Her blonde hair looked like she'd walked through a wind tunnel in a hurricane, but she was still stunning. Only Tory appeared fine. The woman was an icy badass.

Regardless, I was astonished that any of us were still in one piece.

"Down," Candy demanded. "NOW, motherfuckers."

On her command, we all dropped low.

"Did you know it would be like this?" I hissed.

"Yep." Her cheeks were splotched red and sweat beaded her brow. "But it wasn't described as this painful in the damn book."

"More like agonizing," I seethed. "A heads up might have been nice."

Candy adjusted her squat to face me and raised a brow. "Would it have stopped you from coming?"

She had me there. "Nope."

"Then shut your fuckin' cakehole," she shot back. Candy Vargo's attention snapped to Prue. "Stop time. Freeze everything except the seven of us. Can you do that?"

She nodded jerkily. Candy heaved a huge sigh of relief.

I gasped. I'd forgotten that my Angel sisters and brothers had that ability. When they'd first arrived on Earth, they were still doing Zadkiel's dirty work and had tried to destroy me. All four of my siblings had frozen time and did their best to terminate me. They'd failed. What had followed was a difficult road to both trust and love. They had earned mine and I'd earned theirs.

Prue extended her hands and chanted in a dead language. The floor beneath us trembled but didn't give way. A golden mist floated on the air then settled on the ground. "Done," she said.

"Can we stand up if time is frozen?" I asked.

Candy Vargo squinted at me. "Are your legs broken, jackass?"

"No, shit-for-brains," I snapped. "I'm referring to the lasers. Do you think they're frozen too?"

"Only one way to find out," she said, standing up. "Yep. Frozen."

I wanted to punch her in the head. I didn't.

"The lasers are connected to the electricity in the house," Candy said. "Or they were in the book."

"That's kind of dumb," I pointed out. "Anyone could just cut the electric and turn them off."

"Micky Muggles is missing brain cells," Tory reminded me. "He wrote the logistical dragon parts based on his pathetic life. Idiotic people do idiotic things."

"And thank the heavens above for that," Lura Belle said. "If you play stupid games, you win stupid prizes."

I agreed.

"Is there a breaker box in the house?" Dimple asked.

I nodded. "In the kitchen, but I'm not sure we're able to leave this room. Gideon and Gabe couldn't. Every door they went through led right back to the living room."

"Watch me," Dimple said. "I've been goin' places I'm not

wanted my entire dang life. No one is keeping me out of the kitchen."

"Take these," Tory said, clapping her hands and conjuring up tools. She handed Dimple thick rubber gloves, goggles and a blow torch. "It's a bit more permanent than flipping all the switches."

"Been there. Done that," Dimple said with a mortified expression.

"Yep," Jolly Sue confirmed. "Remember when all the Christmas lights in town mysteriously went out at the same time and all the trees blew up during the Holly Days Parade?"

"I do. It was awful. It was a miracle no one died," I said, narrowing my eyes at her. "That happened because Dimple set the fuse box on fire?"

"Yes and no," Lura Belle said, looking mighty guilty. "The power outage was all Dimple. The explosions were someone else."

"Named?" I pressed.

"Lura Belle," the culprit in question admitted. "We weren't invited to sing a solo with the choir. I didn't think that was fair, so I made sure that no one could sing a damn solo."

"You three are batshit crazy," Candy Vargo said.

"Pot, kettle, black," Prue muttered, then focused on Dimple. "Move it. Time will resume in ten minutes, give or take a few."

Dimple hustled toward the kitchen. Surprisingly, or maybe not, she had no problem entering the room. A Nephilim had cast the spell on the Immortals. It was

Nephilim friendly and Immortal hostile. It occurred to me that the old gals might have free rein of the house. Maybe we all would since Micky Muggles hadn't brought us here. We'd come of our own free will. However, there was no time to test the theory.

"Blur your eyes," I demanded. "Look for Gideon, Gabe, Zander, Catriona and Zadkiel."

"What about that sumbitch Micky Muggles?" Lura Belle asked.

I shuddered. "Him too."

Blurring my eyes, I scanned the room. What I saw made me ill. Zander and Catriona lay passed out huddled together where the couch should have been. Both were bloody, broken and beaten. Gabe was a few feet away from them in even worse shape. My brother looked dead. His skin was gray and his eyes were open and staring unseeingly. The ghost of Zadkiel was literally in pieces. His legs and arms were in a pile near the fireplace. His torso and head were on the other side of the room near the stairs.

And Gideon… he was a shell of his former beautiful self. His lips were bluish and his blond hair was matted with blood. The scream of fury that left my throat was only matched by Tory's as she spotted Gabe.

"Are we too fuckin' late?" Candy Vargo shrieked.

"No," I ground out. Saying it made it true. I prayed harder than I'd ever prayed. Plus, if they were dead, I would see their ghosts. Right?

"Well, lookie what I found," Lura Belle snarled.

I turned on a dime and faced the direction her voice had come from. Micky Muggles was frozen like an ice statue.

The scum stood in the entry way to the kitchen. I was surprised Dimple hadn't mowed him down when she took out the fuse box. His ugly mouth was set in a smug grin. I was about to wipe that expression off his face permanently.

"Box destroyed," Dimple yelled, avoiding the monster on her way back.

"Prue, be ready to infuse. Start with Gideon, then go to Gabe. After that, work on Zander then Catriona. I need the strongest healed first."

"What about Zadkiel?" Candy asked, staring at his torso with an expression of disgust and hatred.

My sense of right and wrong wouldn't allow me to say what I was tempted to say. And if he'd truly helped the others here, he deserved for us to try and help him. "Zadkiel is last." I glanced at Prue. "Will you be able to bring yourself to help him?"

Prue ran her hands through her hair in angst. "I can try."

The hate ran deep. Zadkiel deserved it. He'd earned it. Prue was being honest. I refused to fault her for that. "Fine," I said. "Go to Gideon, please."

"On it," she said, squatting down next to Gideon. "The time freeze is about to wear off. I can feel it slipping."

"Tory, go invisible," I ordered. "Stay with me."

"Done," she said tightly. She disappeared without a sound. "I'm right next to you."

I nodded tersely. "Candy Vargo, cover Prue. Make sure she stays safe."

"Good thinkin' motherfucker," she said and sprinted across the room. "You need me, just say the word."

The word... Shit, I needed to share the safe-word

Gideon and I had come up with just in case Micky Muggles assumed one of our bodies. "Listen carefully," I said. "The safe word is toothpick. There's a chance that Micky Muggles will take over one of our bodies. If you believe that to be the case, ask the person the safe word. Do *not* say it aloud. Whisper it. If Micky knows what we're doing we're screwed. Got it?"

"I've got it," Lura Belle grunted. "But we ain't gonna need it. I'm biting some ugly ass shortly."

"With you, sister," Jolly Sue shouted. "I'm hungry for some rump roast!"

"Amen to that!" Dimple bellowed. "I'm ready to snack on some badonkadonk! We're gonna take that sumbitch's magic and give him a Nephilim smackdown he won't forget."

Candy Vargo cackled. "You freaks are fuckin' nuts."

I wasn't sure that biting his ass off was going to be successful. Micky had the power of five Immortals. "Scrap the ass biting," I instructed. "I want you to mess with his mind. Use your powers. Dimple, turn his luck bad. Lura Belle, make him see the worst in himself. And Jolly Sue…" She made people act on their worst impulses. We certainly didn't need that. "Can you just back your sisters up and not use your power?"

"Sure can," she said. "I happen to know lots of embarrassing crap about the cretin. I'm gonna fill him in."

I didn't see how that was going to help, but as long as she didn't encourage him to act on his shitty impulses, I was good.

"I'll take care of removing the dragon's tail," I said in a

brook no bullshit tone. "You gals will put a healthy distance between you and him. Clear?"

"Roger," Dimple said, rubbing her hands together. "Bastard's not gonna know what hit him."

"Wait." I scanned the room. This wasn't the place to go after the dragon. His hoard was in here. "Shove him into the kitchen. I don't want him to know what Prue's doing."

"Genius," Tory said.

The old ladies didn't hesitate. With the magic in them, they had Immortal strength. The shoved Micky Muggles into the kitchen with violent gusto. I knew that Zadkiel wouldn't remove the evil gifts he'd bestowed on them, but I would. They were proving themselves beyond any doubt in my mind."

"Seconds away," Prue warned. "We're almost back in real time."

I stole one quick look at the love of my life then turned my attention back to the piece of shit that tried to steal him from me. I raced into the kitchen. Thankfully, it worked. My eyes had turned gold and my entire body sparked like a firework. I felt Tory's hand on my back. The Nephilim were crouched down and ready to attack.

Micky Muggles was going down.

CHAPTER TEN

Micky Muggles' roar of fury when he realized his hoard had been breached shook the house on its foundation. Thin fissures raced up the walls as they cracked, and chunks of plaster fell from the ceiling. I hoped to heck and back that the same damage wasn't happening on our plane of reality, but if it was... it was. My house was already a wreck.

The *dragon* was hopped up on so much Immortal magic that the freak had wings. They were scraggly, limp and dull brown, but they were there. His roar slowly changed and became a series of yips and shrieks. The pitch was high and manic—something between a prehistoric animal and a dying pack of hyenas.

Not good.

Even if we removed his tail, it would regenerate immediately. He was too Immortal at the moment.

When he spotted me, his beady eyes narrowed, and he

began to laugh. "I reckon this is my lucky day, Daisy... or should I call you Angel of Mercy? You just made my life a whole lot easier. It's sure nice to see ya, but I wouldn't wanna be ya," he bellowed with glee. His hysterics were so out of control that he had to grab the kitchen counter so he didn't fall down. The imbecile banged his head over and over on the granite and congratulated himself repeatedly for getting the prime prize for his hoard. His mind was pretty much gone, which made him even more dangerous.

He continued to bang his head. The crunch and gush of blood when he broke his nose was sickening. The fast rate at which he healed was a terrible sign.

Looking down at the ground, I whispered to Tory. "I'm going to have to fight him to drain his power. When there's an opening, I want you to push him out of the kitchen door and into the yard."

"Done," she whispered.

"Then drop a ward around the house. The Nephilim stay inside. Do not let me back in unless I tell you the safe word."

"As you wish," she replied.

Micky Muggles calmed down after a few minutes and took in the occupants of the room. The idiot believed there were only four people in the kitchen. He was wrong. There were five. One was invisible. He also believed that Dimple, Jolly Sue and Lura Belle were weak and powerless. Again, he was wrong.

"Ain't this just the bee's knees," he snarled, glaring at the three old women. "I'm gonna get me some superpowers and have the pleasure of killin' the bitches who've chapped my ass for decades. Good times."

"Good luck with that, you egg-sucking, dankish, knotty-pated miscreant," Dimple ground out.

Micky Muggles was confused. Not a surprise. He'd flunked out of high school three times before he'd graduated.

"SHUT UP," he hissed at Dimple. "I'm in charge here. This is my territory. I created it. I rule it. And soon," he said, his ego more abundant than his stupidity, "I'll rule every-thing. Forever."

The insane man loved to hear himself talk, but in this, he was grossly mistaken. It was unclear how long his stolen power would last. However, the problem was that there were several very powerful Immortals present—myself included. What I needed to know was how he drained the magic in the first place. Getting myself drained wasn't on my list of things to do. Knowledge was a power more often times stronger than magic.

I kept my gaze trained on the pig. Buying time by tricking him into monologuing might not deplete his magic, but it would give Prue more time to work on Gideon and the others. No matter how much Micky had stolen, there was no way he could go up against all of us at full strength. At least, I hoped not.

Out of the corner of my eye, I noticed Dimple and Lura Belle press their hands together in what looked like prayer. Both of the women's irises had turned white, and their faces were turning red and sweaty. Dimple foamed at the mouth. Lura Belle's nose and ears twitched spastically. A dull yellow haze circled the three Nephilim as Jolly Sue stood behind her sisters and massaged their necks. For a brief moment, I thought they were morphing into zombies. But no.

They weren't zombies.

They weren't praying.

It was something else entirely.

They were summoning their gifts.

The sight wasn't a pretty one, but to me it was beautiful.

Keeping Micky's focus on me was the game right now. I wasn't sure how much damage the gals could do, but if it kept him out of the living room, I was all in.

"How did you do it?" I asked.

"Wouldn't you like to know," he said with a leer as he grabbed his crotch and winked.

I shrugged and stayed neutral even though I would have preferred to gag. "If I'm about to die, I think it's only fair for me to hear your secrets."

He continued to massage his crotch as he considered my request. I knew it would be impossible for him not to brag, so I helped him out.

"My guess is that it's all from Agnes' imagination," I told him. "You never could have come up with something as brilliant as this."

"IT'S ME," he yelled as spittle flew from his lips. "It was all me. Agnes would be nothing without me."

"Would have been," I corrected him. "You killed her."

"I did," he said with a satisfied smirk. "Had to. She killed me first. Fair is fair."

"That was fiction," I replied coolly. "What you did was real."

His unattractive face screwed up into a fake expression

of remorse. "Come on, Daisy," he said. "You know as well as I do that humans are scum. No need for them."

"You're human," I reminded him.

"Not anymore," he announced grandly. He splayed his arms wide, and his crappy, misshapen wings fluttered. He was so thrilled he hadn't noticed they were molting. Washed-out brown feathers shed and fell to the floor. The skeletal frame of his wings was showing. The bones were aged, brittle and deteriorating. I could break them with a flick of my fingers, no magic necessary. I was so very tempted, but I held back.

It wasn't time yet.

"I shoulda been Immortal all along," he griped. "Zadkiel had the power to make me in his image, but he pussied out. I figure he knew I'd be stronger than him." He chucked and stroked his mangy wings. "Guess the joke's on him now."

I sucked in a breath and wondered if I'd misconstrued what he'd just implied. Had Zadkiel sired Micky Muggles as well as Dimple, Jolly Sue and Lura Belle? If so, they were related. That family tree was a shitshow.

The self-proclaimed dragon was getting antsy. It was time for a different tactic—caring and compassionate. It wasn't for him. It was for the Immortals in the living room and for my daughter. If Gideon left me alone in this world because of Micky Muggles, I was going to have my revenge. I'd happily swallow fire for Gideon. Pretending concern wasn't a biggie.

"Oh, Micky," I said, forcing my expression to one of tenderness and pity. "I didn't realize that horrible man was your father. My condolences. I despise him too." He wasn't sure if I was pulling his leg or being honest. He was stupid and vain. I'd just push a little more. "You're so much better looking than him."

It was a blatant untruth. Zadkiel might personify evil, but his outward shell had been stunning. Micky Muggles was not stunning. With his mullet and beer belly, he was the perfect picture of a redneck loser.

"Well now," he said, flexing his scrawny muscles. "I do believe you're right. I've banged a whole hell of a lot of big-tittied women in my day." He looked me up and down like I was a piece of meat and he was starving. "Wouldn't mind addin' you to the collection."

"To be determined," I replied coyly. The words felt like sandpaper in my mouth, but I kept going. "I might be inclined if you tell me how you created this wonderful hoard and got so sexy and powerful."

He chuckled and rocked his hips forward. Lura Belle's white eyes began to glow silver, and Micky grabbed his head in pain.

"My dick is tiny," he shouted, much to his confusion and horror. "I ain't never satisfied a woman in my life."

He shook his head rapidly as if he was trying to expel the admission from his mind. He took two steps towards me and then tripped over his feet as Dimple's eyes matched her sister's. One of his wings broke off, and he began to swear. Dimple and Lura Belle smiled. They were just getting started.

The Collector, as he was known in the Immortal world, slapped his hands over his mouth in terror as words began spilling out. He didn't succeed in halting them. "My ex-wife kicked me to the curb 'cause I couldn't get it up no more. Hurt my feelings."

"I'm so sorry to hear that," I told him.

"LIES!" he bellowed. "My pecker is a legend."

I nodded kindly. "I'm sure it is. So, tell me about your dad."

"He ain't no dad," Micky snarled. "Zadkiel's a fuckin' sperm donor."

I stopped myself before I could ask him if his pun was accidental or intended. Micky Muggles wouldn't understand. I smiled and hoped it didn't look like a wince. "I know what it's like growing up without a father. I'm so sorry."

"I'm not," he said with an oily laugh. "That bastard didn't give me Immortality, so I took it. Laugh's on him. He's dang close to turnin' to dust. Been lookin' forward to this day for a long time."

"How old are you, if you don't mind me asking?" I asked, purely out of curiosity. A Nephilim's life was longer than a human's lifespan, but from what Charlie had said, the *Collector* had been around a very long time.

"Couple thousand—extended my years just bidin' my time and waitin' for my day," he answered with great pride. "Been takin' what's mine for centuries."

I tilted my head to the side. "But was it? Was it really yours to take?"

"I have a blow-up doll," he shouted. "I named her Canker."

My lips compressed, and I bit down on the inside of my cheek so I didn't laugh. It was as if the gals had infected him with truth serum. Micky began to throw a tantrum. He stomped around the kitchen, but due to Dimple's gift, he kept tripping. His one remaining wing hung limply from his back, but every cut and wound he received from his falls healed quickly.

He was still too strong to remove his tail.

"It's okay, Micky," I said, watching as he got closer to the door leading outside. "I'm not judging."

"Her name ain't Canker," he ground out, looking wild-eyed and manic. "Her name is Smidget, and she don't talk back or make fun of my miniscule man-meat."

He froze. His face turned ashy white.

"It ain't miniscule," he screamed as he began to violently punch himself in the head.

I was very wrong to think the gals wouldn't be helpful. I thanked my lucky stars that their gifts didn't work on Immortals. They were terrifying.

While Micky might believe he was both a dragon and an Immortal, he was a Nephilim. He always had been and always would be until he was dead… which was going to happen shortly.

"I've heard it's huge," I said.

He calmed immediately. I gave a discreet nod to the gals to tamp it back. They got the memo.

"It is," he claimed, pointing to his crotch. "You wanna see it?"

My gag was internal, but very strong. "Not quite yet. I find your brilliance in creating the hoard very arousing. If you'd truly like to get me in the mood, tell me all about it."

He grinned and rotated his hips in a lewd way. I ignored the repulsive move and kept my eyes on his face.

"It weren't nothin'," he bragged. "Since you're gonna be dead soon—after I bang your brains out—I might as well tell ya." The maggot of a man leaned back on the counter and wiggled his pointer finger. It lit up with a small flame. "Figured a little candlelight might be right nice."

I was repulsed but didn't let it show. "I love candles."

"Thought so," he said, lighting up all ten of his fingers.

It would be all kinds of karmically wonderful if the idiot set himself on fire. Sadly, with his power level still being high, it wouldn't end him. I wasn't worried. Ending him was my job... and I was going to be thorough.

"Well now," he began. "I'll give a little credit to old Agnes. I didn't know nothin' about dragons until I listened to one of her books on tape about twenty years back. But when I heard them words, I finally knew what I was after all this time. I'd been collectin' things for centuries—money, cars, women and magic. I'm a dragon."

"Wow," I said. "Is that when you started being her handyman?"

He seemed surprised that I was aware of his and Agnes' relationship. I didn't want to piss him off, so I didn't reveal anything else.

"It was," he replied, still slightly guarded.

"Brilliant," I lied. "Your mind is astounding."

He bought the bullshit and kept going. "Yep, that's what I say too. The hoard was the easy part. Long time ago, I heard about them portals y'all use to get to the Light and the

Darkness. Tried like a house on fire to get to the Light to kill Zadkiel."

"Who told you about the portals?" I asked.

"Some dumbass who was beggin' for his life when I drained him," he said with an arrogance so disturbing it was difficult not to electrocute him. "I told him I'd let him go if he told me a secret. He did... and I didn't."

"Ballsy," I said, biting back all my instincts to end him where he stood.

If I went for him in the house, it was a danger to Gideon and everyone else. I was furious, but I wasn't stupid. That honor went to Micky Muggles.

"Funny thing was," he continued, "when I tried to get to the portals it didn't work out. But somethin' better did."

"You discovered how to create a parallel plane?"

"Bingo," he said with a grin.

Of all the dumb and deadly luck...

"That's amazing," I lied. "What about the siphoning of power? Did you learn that from an Immortal as well?"

"Hell to the no," he said with a laugh that made my stomach churn. "Figured that out all by myself."

I stayed silent and waited. There was no way he wasn't going to tell me. The man needed validation like a fire needed oxygen. His conceit knew no bounds.

"You ever heard of a vampire?" he asked.

"Umm... yep. They're fiction."

"You might think so," he replied with a smarmy grin. "But that ain't true."

"Go on," I said, doing a little shimmy to show my enthusiasm.

Again, the perverted pig bought it.

"Happened by accident," he explained. "Found me an Immortal who I was gonna rob. Rich as Midas. When I was takin' what I deserved, he caught me. But I was prepared. My gift is fire along with being able to morph into other bodies," he told me nodding to his flaming fingers. "Turned me into a pyro, but I kinda liked it. I set that there Immortal on fire, and when he tried to put it out, I lopped his fool head off with a sword. Blood everywhere." The joyous glint in his eyes was abhorrent. His lack of value for life was psychotic. "I got the goods and was makin' my getaway. Funny thing though... I slipped in all that blood, and some of it got into my mouth. The rush that went through me was somethin' I'll never forget."

"And you realized it gave you magic?"

"Nah, not right then," he shared. "But I liked that rush so much, I stayed and drank that bastard dry. Taste ain't all that great, but no pain, no gain."

I nodded. If I spoke, I would scream. The fact that he'd come upon everything by dumb luck was hard to believe.

"Wasn't until after about a hundred years or so I realized that drinkin' all that blood made my life longer. I still looked like I was in my thirties and could age even younger the more I drank." He chuckled and gave me a flaming thumbs up. "I was stronger after each sip and it became easier to find and kill the others."

"You don't feel bad about that?" I questioned, wondering if there was even an ounce of humanity inside him.

"Hell no," he said with a burst of laughter. "It's a dog-eat-dog world, Angel of Mercy. I'd rather be the dog with a full belly than roadkill."

He was more nauseating than any roadkill I'd ever seen. Telling him wouldn't go over well.

"Interesting," I said as my mind raced with disgusting possibilities. If what he said was true and it appeared to be so, I could take his power if I bit him and drank his blood. Even the thought of it made me want to hurl.

However, it didn't seem to make Dimple, Jolly Sue or Lura Belle ill. There were gnashing their teeth and licking their lips. Shit. The information Micky Muggles had just shared was bad in every sense of the word. I wasn't sure if it was the chance at getting a few fleeting moments of Immortality that was attractive to the old gals or if they just saw it as a way to get rid of the disease named Micky Muggles. Either way, we were *not* going to test that theory unless it was a last resort.

The new game was to get the low-life out of the house and wear his power down. Micky might have stolen a tremendous amount of magic, but I had a tremendous amount of my own. Plus, even though Gideon and Abaddon had said it would fade, I still had the dark magic running through my bloodstream. Micky had fucked around and he was about to find out.

"Door. Now," I said to my invisible friend.

Micky glared at me in confusion. "What?"

There was no time to answer. Tory worked fast and with precision. The concealed force of the woman known as Purgatory hit Micky Muggles so hard, he screamed. As he flew out of the door and into the yard with a look of pure shock on his face, I laughed.

"Stay," I said to the Nephilim. "This is my fight. Go help Candy Vargo."

Amazingly, they didn't argue. They didn't hurl any sixteenth century insults at me. They hightailed it back to the living room. There was no time to check on Prue's progress. Gideon, Gabe and the others were in terrible shape. My sister had her work cut out for her.

So did I.

I expected her to succeed. There was no other alternative.

I planned to succeed as well.

"I'm coming, Micky," I called out as I sprinted out of the house. "And you're going to get plowed, only, not in the way you were hoping for. Guess the last laugh will be on you after all."

CHAPTER ELEVEN

Tory had not messed around. She'd thrown the dirtbag at least two hundred feet. He was not happy. As I stalked out the door after him, I looked around the area that Micky Muggles had claimed as his lair. The property looked identical to the area Gideon and I had built our home for our family. The place where we'd decided to raise our daughter. The foundation had been strong but seeing it on this plane of existence was like swallowing bitter ash. Clearly, I knew this land wasn't our land. There were no stars, moon or clouds in the sky, just an ominous darkness. An eerie and unsettling quiet blanketed the landscape. Still, the rage inside me burned without care of consequences.

I knew that was foolish and reckless.

According to Tim, the writer William Inge wrote —'There are no rewards or punishments—only consequences.' It was logical and profound. Pushing down the rage was hard, but anger would make me sloppy.

I am the Angel of Mercy.

I am the Death Counselor.

I am a partner to someone I love beyond reason.

I am a mother.

Being sloppy was unacceptable.

I focused on my surroundings. Upon closer inspection, the trees looked brittle and their branches drooped. The air felt clammy and smelled slightly acrid. It seemed Micky's parallel plane was falling apart... just like his wings.

The slight rumble behind me let me know that Tory had put up a ward around the house. I breathed a sigh of relief and eyed my objective.

"You want to know what I think would be fun?" I shouted as he got to his feet.

His movements were jerky as he shook his fists in the air. "You will not disrespect me!" he bellowed.

"Whatever do you mean?" I asked innocently. He'd caused so much pain to so many that I took a small delight in his outraged confusion at his ass being ousted.

"You did something," he snarled and beat his fists against his thighs like a petulant child. "I'm the ruler here. Not you."

Holding up my hands in a sign of surrender, I laughed. "On my Immortal life, I didn't do that."

The truth was always easier to remember than a lie. I hadn't lied at all. I didn't send him flying out of the house. I might have given the order, but I didn't do the deed.

Micky Muggles wasn't sure what to think. He stomped his foot and glared. "I don't believe you."

I scratched my head in mock confusion and squinted at him. "Wait. Are you telling me you didn't do that yourself?

Because I found it very sexy. I've never seen an Immortal blast out of a house before. I'm pretty sure I've never seen an Immortal fly. Those wings of yours must come in handy."

The idiot was bewildered. He paced erratically and muttered to himself. Losing one's mind wasn't a pretty business. When he finished working through whatever was happening in his pea-sized brain, he stilled and gave me his most charming smile.

It wasn't charming. It was slimy and demented.

"My bad," he said with a chuckle. "I'm so dang powerful, sometimes I do shit and don't even know I did it. Can you believe that?"

"Wow. Crazy!"

He ambled toward me and bared his teeth. The idiot was a little less than half a football field away, but I could see his mouth clearly. His teeth were no longer blunt and in need of a good cleaning. They were sharp and fangy. My guess was that he was done playing around. He was ready to drink me dry.

He was in for a surprise. I had no intention of being his blood bank.

"Hold on there, big boy," I said with a wink. "Before we do the deed, how about a friendly little sparring session? You know, for old time's sake."

He paused and eyed me warily. The freak came closer. He stopped fifty feet out. "Whatcha got in mind?"

I shrugged and let my fingers begin to spark. "I just love a man with magic. Do me one last solid before my time is up. Turn me on with your power, Micky Muggles."

He gave me an aww shucks grin that didn't quite work with the razor-sharp fangs. "I'm guessin' that ain't too much to ask." He gyrated his hips in my direction. His pecker popped out of his fly and whirled like a helicopter. "I *do* like to satisfy the ladies."

I was going to buy stock in eye bleach when this was over. I forced a smile that felt like a grimace. "That's what I hear," I told him. "Can I take the first shot, sexy guy?"

"Be my guest," he said with a bravado that I was going to make him eat. "Give it your best shot, Daisy. Cause I ain't gonna hold back even though you're just a girl."

"As you wish," I replied, using the phrase that my Immortal friends liked to say. It felt right and rolled right off my tongue with ease.

The goal was to wear down his magic. Any damage I did to him now could be repaired. Aware of that, I raised my hands in the air and slashed them down to my sides. I smacked him so hard with a bolt of electricity that it sent him flying into a tree. It was the kind of blast that would have made Candy Vargo laugh and call me a weenie. Not so much with Micky Muggles.

"I bet your mamma felt that one," I muttered.

The look of utter shock on his face told me several things. He might have the power, but he'd never really been in a fight with an Immortal. Hope surged through me. If he didn't know how to fight, I had the upper hand.

The fact that he possessed the magic of the Grim Reaper, the Archangel, Zander, Catriona and whatever he was able to extract from Zadkiel was insane. The fact that he didn't know how to use it... priceless.

Until it wasn't.

Huge orbs of rapid-fire fiery cannonballs flew at me. Not good. I had little time to do much but duck and weave to avoid getting blasted. Luckily, his aim was terrible.

I quickly sprinted away from the house when he landed a blast far too close to my home for comfort.

When I got my bearings, I matched him shot for shot. His fireballs might've been more powerful than my bolts of lightning, but unlucky for him, I landed all of mine.

Even so, his healing time was impressive which meant he was still juiced up to the gills with Immortal magic.

He'd only grazed me with a few fireballs. Nothing I couldn't instantly remedy. However, the craters he caused in the yard could house ten Olympic sized swimming pools. Avoiding the enormous holes in the ground was more difficult than dodging his crappily thrown counterattacks.

"You gonna die, bitch," he screeched as I deflected one of his fireballs and sent it back his way.

"Not today," I taunted him. "You couldn't hit the broad side of a barn if you were standing right next to it."

Frantic banging on the bubble behind me caught my attention. Looking over my shoulder was a mistake. In the brief second it took to see what was happening, Micky Muggles landed a shot. My entire body went up in searing magical flames. The heat was so intense I wondered if my skin was melting off my body.

I had thought he was tiring. It had been a premature conclusion. My shit-talk must've given him a second wind, and I was paying a scorching price. My bad. Hindsight is 20/20...

However, what I'd observed on the other side of the ward filled my heart with joy. Gideon, Gabe, Zander, Catriona, Candy Vargo, Prue, Tory, Dimple, Lura Belle and Jolly Sue stood together. None of the Immortals who'd been in the hoard appeared to be completely healed, but they were alive. Gideon looked as if he was about to implode. His eyes were a blazing red and sparkled with fury. His fists were as clenched as his steel-cut jaw.

He was gorgeous.

As the fire consumed me, I tried to put it out. I was only able to clear my face of the flames, but it was all I needed. Tory's gaze burned into mine as I heard Micky Muggles gloating about killing me dead. I shouted the safe word. "Toothpick," I cried out.

Tory slashed her arms through the air in a circular motion. Her silver hair blew around her head and her piercing blue eyes shone like diamonds in the dark night. The ward disintegrated into millions of icy crystals and I was no longer on my own.

Zander, Catriona, Candy Vargo and Gabe ran at Micky Muggles like bombs out of a cannon. Dimple, Lura Belle and Jolly Sue were right on their tail. I wanted to stop them, but Gideon dove on top of me to roll out the flames. Prue and Tory stood by to keep us safe and block any shot Micky threw at us. The Grim Reaper chanted in a foreign tongue and I felt his power seep into me and become one with mine. Slowly the fire receded and my body became whole.

"Am I dead?" I asked, coughing then inhaling deeply. I patted my body checking for missing and chard parts. Everything felt...normal. Looking down at myself, I gasped.

My clothes were intact along with the rest of me, and I could still feel the hair on my head. I quickly mashed my palms to my face. It was still there. My man had some powerful healing mojo. I beamed up at Gideon with a smile that I hoped conveyed all the love I held for him.

"Dammit, Death Counselor," he choked out. He rested his forehead on mine now that the fire was fully extinguished. "That took fucking years off my life."

"Not sure it matters," I said with a weak laugh, cupping his cheek in my hand. "You're Immortal, Reaper."

He kissed me, and his lips on mine were a balm to my soul. The kiss wasn't gentle. It was rough, deep and life affirming. It was necessary for both of us. I kissed him back as if my life depended on it. His insistent lips made me dizzy with lust. I was sure I'd forgotten my own name. I'd definitely forgotten what was going on around us.

"Get a room, dummies," Prue said, separating us and checking me over quickly.

Reality came back with a punch to the gut as I heard Dimple scream.

"Shit," I said, trying to get up to run.

My legs gave out. Gideon caught me as I started to fall. While Micky Muggles hadn't succeeded in ending me, he'd hit me with the combined magic of some of the most powerful Immortals alive. It hadn't been a walk in the park, and I wasn't a hundred percent by any stretch of the imagination.

Tory laid her hands on my shoulders. I felt her healing magic penetrate my skin and wind through me like a tendril of light. It was warm and gentle as it seeped into my veins.

"Better?" she asked, searching my eyes frantically.

I tested my legs. "Much," I told her. "Go, go, go. Help the others."

She nodded curtly then sprinted to Gabe's side. He put his back to hers and they fought the enemy together like a well-honed weapon. Tory's silver and Gabe's gold blended as their power united. It was magnificent to behold.

Prue had followed Tory, but stood on the other side of our brother, helping Zander and Catriona with their assault. No one was at full strength except those of us who hadn't been imprisoned, so I was happy to see Prue and Tory lending their strength to the others.

Even so, the imbalance in the magic gave Micky Muggles a slight upper hand on our crew. He focused on the ones he knew were weaker.

When I tried to join in the foray, Gideon wrapped his arms around me from behind.

"We're staying here," he said in a tone that dared me to defy him. "You're in no shape to fight. They have it covered."

"I can't just do nothing," I told him. "They've all risked their lives to help me. To help us."

Gideon eased his grip, but before I could slip out, Candy Vargo shouted, "Get the fuckin' tail!" The demand in her voice was so loud the trees lost the few dried up leaves they still held. She glowed a brilliant orange and wasn't screwing around. "Gotta cut off the dragons tail."

"What tail?" Zander growled as he threw another weak ball of magic at the false dragon.

"On it!" Lura Belle shrieked. "Sumbitch is going down."

The dragon hadn't paid a lick of attention to the

Nephilim. He hadn't thought of them as a threat. In his eyes, they were nothing.

No one ever said that Micky Muggles was smart.

I watched Dimple, Jolly Sue and Lura Belle sneak around and get behind the evil bastard. I winced when they almost got nailed by a lightning bolt sent over by Candy Vargo. The three old crazy women huddled together and waited for their opening. Under Lura Belle's direction they carefully approached the dragon's tail. Everyone on the other side either knew what was happening or thought the Nephilim had lost their minds.

"What the hell?" Gideon asked.

"Just wait," I said.

"REMOVE THE ASS!" Lura Belle shouted.

The dragon, fool that he was, hadn't seen them coming. The trio of gals launched themselves at the mullet-sporting jerk and yanked his pants down to his knees. Dimple kicked him in the back, and he fell forward, his face smashing into the dusty ground with a satisfying thud. That's when the three of them, like rabid dogs, bit Micky Muggles ass right off of his scrawny body. He shrieked and did his best to shake them off. But there was no stopping three furious old biddies from the job they had to do. I'd never seen anything like it, and I hoped to never see it again.

Dimple stood up with a large section of Micky Muggles ass in her mouth. The Nephilim looked as if she'd been bludgeoned, but the blood and ripped flesh was all fake dragon butt. The old woman pumped her wrinkled fists over her head in victory.

Her sisters joined in the celebration as the rest of us watched with a mixture of horror and mad respect.

"This is for being a beetle-headed, boar-pig shit-ass," Jolly Sue snarled at the profusely bleeding Micky Muggles before kicking him in the head. She, too, had a mouthful of dragon tail and blood all over her. However, it was Lura Belle who came out on top... if you could call it that.

The self-proclaimed leader of the trio had ass in her mouth and both of her hands. She was by far the bloodiest of the three. It was repulsive. She didn't think so. She grinned and spit the butt out of her mouth. "That dragon ain't got no tail anymore!"

"Holy fuck!" Candy Vargo shouted with a guttural laugh. "Three cheers for the badass bitches!" She tossed a box of toothpicks to Lura Belle. "You're definitely going to need these after that." She then approached the assless Micky Muggles. "What do we want to do with him?"

"Purgatory," Tory said coldly. "I believe he should stay there until a more *permanent* solution is found."

"Fuck you," Micky Muggles howled. "Ain't no such thing as Purgatory."

Tory simply smiled. It was seriously scary. Micky Muggles tried to crawl away, but Gabe stepped on his shirt.

My brother squatted down and got in the dragon's face. He placed his hand on his neck and squeezed. "Do not ever backtalk Tory again," he said in a tone that made Micky Muggles whimper. "Purgatory will be a nice little vacation before you go to your final resting place. "Trust me on that. Payment for what you've done will be everlasting."

Gideon walked over to the piece of shit on the ground.

His fury was obvious in his measured movement and the fire spitting from his eyes. Micky covered his head in terror. "He's mine after his stint in Purgatory. Am I clear?" Gideon ground out.

"Very," Tory replied then glanced over at me. "Shall I take him now?"

"Can you get him there from this plane or do we need to take him back to the mortal plane?" I asked. From the way Micky was bleeding out, I wasn't sure he would survive the trip back. Honestly, I didn't care.

"I can get to Purgatory from anywhere in the Universe," she said in an emotionless voice. "It's my home."

"I'm coming with you," Gabe said, walking over to her and extending his hand.

She stared at it for a long beat then took it in hers. "I can't let you do that."

"I can't let you go alone," he replied softly.

"You have to," she said, letting go of him and stepping away.

A pop, loud and unexpected, startled us. Putrid green smoke filled the air, and the scent made my eyes water. When the smoke cleared, Micky Muggles was gone. In the wind we heard, "See ya. Wouldn't wanna be ya. But no worries, I'll be seein' y'all soon."

"What the actual fuck?" Candy Vargo shouted. "Did that fucker just up and vanish?"

"He did," Gideon said in a flat tone that made the hair on the back of my neck stand up. "He played us. He still has a little power left."

"Not a problem," Dimple assured the enraged group.

"We've got his ass. He can't store anymore magic. The weedy, whey-faced bum-bailey is done."

Lura Belle, with blood dripping off her chin and a tooth-pick hanging out of her mouth, agreed. "Yep. My guess is that the onion-eyed wagtail will become his true age when the rest of the magic wears off. That sumbitch is a Nephilim. He said it himself that he's been alive a few thousand years. That shit isn't gonna fly when we've got his tail." She held up what looked like a raw piece of hanger steak.

It was repulsively beautiful. The dragon had lost his tail. He had no way to store his stolen magic now. Granted, he could drain someone to buy more time, but he'd have to do it so often he'd leave a nasty trail. It would be easy to follow.

Candy Vargo circled the area where Micky Muggles had been only moments ago. "I don't like this. That jackass is smarter than we think. I want Charlie's opinion."

"Agreed," Gideon said, putting his arm around me. "I think we should leave this hellish place."

"I am so good with that," I replied, resting my head on his shoulder.

Tory held up a pale hand. "We have unfinished business here."

I glanced over at Prue. "Were you able to revive Zadkiel?"

"Yes," she said flatly. "He doesn't have long though. I'm not sure he'll ever leave this plane."

"He belongs in Purgatory," Tory snapped. "He will suffer like the Martyrs. Period."

There had been enough fighting. Stepping in between

Prue and Tory, I placed a hand on each of their arms. "Let's go assess the situation and figure it out from there."

En masse we walked back into the home that Gideon and I had built that wasn't our home at all. It was time to take care of the unfinished business.

CHAPTER TWELVE

THE GHOST OF MY IMMORTAL ENEMY WAS ON THE FLOOR. HE was no longer just a torso. Prue had given him back enough power for his transparent body to become whole. The ex-Angel of Mercy looked abysmal. The deterioration was severe. While his legs and arms were attached, they were hanging by tendons. Zadkiel's face was sunken, and his chest was caving in. I'd been dealing with the dead for a while now. It was my honor and my gift. My compassion for my deceased guests knew no bounds. However, it took all I had to feel any compassion at all for the evil man who had done his best to destroy me and everyone I loved.

All of us stood together in a semi-circle and observed the trash at our feet.

Almost everyone in the room had been at the receiving end of the man's unhinged wrath. Some of the worst of his ungodly behavior had been aimed at my siblings, Prue, Gabe, Abby and Rafe. He'd kept them as slaves and made them absorb the sins of man for centuries. He'd mentally and physically broken them repeatedly. The fact that they were now functioning beings was a miracle. Happiness was the best revenge. As hard as Zadkiel had tried to annihilate my brothers and sisters, in the end, he'd failed.

Good doesn't always outweigh evil, but when it does, it's glorious.

Tory was another of his victims. To say her life had been harsh would be an understatement. Along with my siblings, she'd been tortured and abused. I believed that Zadkiel had loved her, but his love was a poison that killed souls. His jealousy over the union between Tory and Gabe had decimated two lives. The lies that he'd planted had taken root in the ground as the seeds grew into a devastating divide between something that could have been pure and beautiful.

I didn't know if there was any going back for Tory and Gabe, but it was clear that Gabe wanted it. I believed that Tory did as well, but the time that had passed had not been kind.

Most everything that the original Angel of Mercy touched turned to shit. It galled me that, in the end, he wouldn't suffer the consequences of his actions. If the man turned to dust, he would go nowhere—not to Purgatory, the Light or the Darkness. He would simply fade into oblivion. Not that he was destined to the Light at all. While he may have been good millions of years ago, the sins he'd committed over millenniums weighed far more than the good he'd done in the beginning.

"I despise you," Tory said in a flat tone as she stared daggers at the man who had ruined her life.

Zadkiel stared back at her with a vacant expression before he had the audacity to ask for a favor.

"I would like to speak," he whispered. "I need your help."

Purgatory closed her eyes and hissed. Gabe growled like an animal. Tory held up her hand to stop my brother from attacking the man who had violently dismantled their lives.

"This is not for you," she sneered at Zadkiel, waving her hands in the air and sending some healing magic his way. "It's so that the people in this room can rip you to shreds before you turn to ash. They're owed the final word, you vile piece of shit."

Tory stood as still as a statue as she continued to give her tormentor the energy to hear what others wanted to say. It was clear it was taking both a mental and physical toll on her, but Tory defined the term badass. She might seem as cold as ice, but underneath, there was a beating heart full of love screaming to be heard.

"Thank you," Zadkiel said.

She didn't grace him with a reply.

The Nephilim approached Zadkiel. They stood hand in hand and looked down on the man who had mated with human women and sired them. They were covered in blood and gore. The Chanel outfits they wore looked like Halloween zombie costumes. Their normally coiffed hair was a blood-caked mess, and Dimple was missing her sensible pumps. They'd never been more beautiful. Their lives had been filled with anguish due to the gifts their sperm donor had bestowed on them. It was unclear how much time they had left before they died, but at well over a hundred years old, they couldn't have much more.

I didn't know the lifespan of a Nephilim. What I did know was that I was going to make sure the time they had left was filled with joy. If Zadkiel refused to take back the horrendous gifts he'd forced upon them, I would do it. Candy Vargo's ass didn't lie. *The one who giveth can taketh away. Or if denied, maybe the next one can.*

I was the next one. I was the Angel of Mercy now, and I would do right by the women who he'd done wrong. They deserved peace in their final years.

"Take them back," Lura Belle snapped at the ghost on the floor. "You're a piece of crap, and you owe us before you turn to dust."

Again, all Zadkiel did was stare at them vacantly.

"Wake up, you haggard, reeky moldwarp," Dimple ground out. "We've been doing your dirty work for over a century. I'm ashamed to have your rancid blood running through my veins."

Jolly Sue was so red in the face, I thought she might be having a stroke. "Do you know how many times I've tried to end my life, you puny, mewling maggot?" she shouted, trembling like a leaf in the wind.

Lura Belle and Dimple put their age-spotted arms around her.

"It's impossible," Jolly Sue spat. "Not only did you destroy our lives by making us pariahs, you took away the ability for us to end it. The word vile doesn't come close to describing you. You have never been loved and will not be missed. Everything you've ever touched is tainted. The legacy you leave is shameful. You're nothing."

"I sent the message," Zadkiel said. His voice was hoarse and soft.

Candy Vargo eyed him with distrust and fury. "I call bullshit," she ground out.

Zadkiel's head turned to her. I knew that he and Candy had a physical relationship at one time long, long ago. It was something that she regretted. There was no love lost between them. If there had ever been real feelings, they'd died like everything Zadkiel had ever involved himself in.

"I did," he replied.

Candy got down low and in his face. "Tell me what you sent, you lyin' sack of shit. Prove that you sent it, fucker."

His body grew more transparent with each word he spoke. Tory sent more magic. She was pale normally, but she grew paler.

"The one who giveth can taketh away. Or if denied, maybe the next one can," Zadkiel told the Keeper of Fate.

Candy raised a brow and stood back up. "Knock me over with a fuckin' feather," she muttered.

Zadkiel was fading fast, no matter how hard Tory worked to keep him here. If he'd sent the message, there was a reason.

"Make good on your promise," I demanded. "Your cruelty makes you an abomination. Making it right at this point is impossible, but you have the chance to undo some of the harm you've caused."

I glared at the ghost. He'd terrified me at a cellular level for a long time. Now, he was just pathetic. Hatred was a wasted emotion. It took time and space in my heart. Zadkiel didn't deserve to live anywhere in my heart. In a moment of complete clarity, I realized that he didn't anymore. I would never feel love or compassion for the man. Forgiveness wasn't on the agenda either, but I no longer hated him. He deserved nothing from me.

Zadkiel nodded his head. It almost fell off. He raised a feeble and almost completely transparent hand. Making a circular motion, a small amount of golden enchantment trickled in the air around him. "Dimple, Jolly Sue and Lura Belle," he whispered. "I rescind the curses I bestowed upon you. You are no longer under the compulsion to do harm. Go in peace and live the rest of your life in harmony."

The Nephilim began to cry. They didn't go to their father. They didn't thank him. They barely acknowledged him. He'd never been a father figure to the three women. He'd just been a man who had caused them unmeasurable pain.

"As much as it pains me to say it—and it pains me greatly," Gideon said, walking over to Zadkiel and standing in front of him. "I wouldn't be standing here right now if Zadkiel had not given up his magic to me. I am appreciative."

Zadkiel closed what was left of his eyes and gave an almost imperceptible nod to the Grim Reaper. Gideon made his way back to me and held my hand. The solidness and warmth of his touch kept me grounded. He was my rock, and I was his.

Gabe's teeth were gritted, and his fists were clenched by his sides, but he walked over and stood at Zadkiel's feet. "You have gone above and beyond to tear me down and shatter my soul. You did this for thousands of years—to me, my siblings and Tory. God only knows how many others you tortured and dismantled mentally." He ran his hands through his blond hair and sighed. It was the most loaded sigh I'd ever heard. "I could choose to become what I was taught. I could choose to become like you. You beat your vicious lessons into me well. I have scars—both mental and physical from your teachings. However, I choose goodness over evil. It wasn't a lesson you taught. It was one taught to me by people who truly love me."

My brother glanced over at me with a smile that lit his gorgeous golden eyes. It made my heart beat a rapid rhythm. I was sure it was about to burst in my chest. I smiled back at him and tried not to cry. When he mouthed the words, *I love you*, I lost it. Tears of happiness rolled down my cheeks and splashed to the floor. Gideon pulled me close and kissed the top of my head. Zadkiel had failed in the end. For that, I would forever be grateful.

Gabe, the Archangel, turned his attention back to the man on the floor. "I refuse to give you anything. You will never have my love or my respect. However," he paused and glanced over at Tory. She stared right back at him. He gave her a smile she didn't return and he focused back on Zadkiel. "However," he repeated. "I will thank you for giving me what I needed to live. My life without you in it is more than I ever imagined I would have. So again, I thank you for your final gift of contrition."

Zadkiel grew uncomfortable with Gabe's admission of thanks. The horrid man had done the right thing in the very end, but it couldn't make up for all the agony he'd caused.

"I am sorry," he said.

Like Candy Vargo only moments ago, his words could have knocked me over with a feather.

"None of you deserved what I did," he went on, growing weaker and weaker. "I could blame it on the madness that comes with Immortality, but I shall not. That would be a pathetic attempt to escape my deplorable actions. The truth is… I don't know why. I don't know why I did the unspeakable things I did. I don't know why…"

His voice faded off. Parts of his body began to turn to dust. Tory closed her eyes and sent more magic. I was worried she was about to pass out. Gabe went to her and held her up. It was a miracle and possibly a good sign she didn't push him away.

Zander stepped forward. "I don't know you," he said to the ghost. "What I do know is that you helped save my sister and myself. Thank you." With a curt nod to Zadkiel, he walked away and stood right in front of Prue. "And you," he said, marveling at her. "You're a goddess. I'm forever in your debt."

Prue blushed a bright pink and looked down at the floor. Zander reached out, gently cupped her chin and raised her head so their gazes met.

"You're both good and beautiful," he said. "Your beauty is blinding due to the purity of your heart. I vow to protect you and be at your service until the end of time."

"Umm… not necessary," Prue stuttered, blushing even deeper.

"It is," Catriona insisted, taking Prue's hands in hers.

It was the first time I'd heard her speak. She was as stunning as her brother and her voice had a melodic quality that calmed my soul.

"You gave of yourself… to us—people you didn't know," Catriona said as her gaze bounced back and forth between Prue and Zander. Her grin was all-knowing and filled with delight. "We will be lifelong friends."

There was something happening there… Only time would tell if it came to anything. Since we lived forever, time was a currency we had plenty of.

Prue approached Zadkiel. Her face had gone from an alluring pink to ashen. She stared at him with dead eyes. "I speak for myself, Abby and Rafe. You're a despicable animal. The hope and dream of one who lives for hundreds of thousands of years is that someday we'll have lived a good enough life to earn a place in the Light. I'll sleep better at night knowing that you're gone and have no chance at earning any love from the higher power. I refuse to let you live in my nightmares anymore. You don't deserve any of my energy—good or bad. You've taken all you will ever get from me and my brothers and sister. Good riddance to bad rubbish. In the end, you lost."

The room was silent. Candy Vargo walked over to Prue, took her in her arms and hugged her tight. My sister's sobs tore at my heart. The Keeper of Fate whispered in Prue's ear helping her to calm down. Candy might deny she was *nice*, but she was a liar. As profane and mannerless as she was, she had the biggest heart of all.

"It's almost time," Zadkiel said as what remained of him began to slip into the void of nothingness. His attention was on me. I gave him the courtesy of acknowledging him.

"Speak your piece," I said, keeping my tone and expression neutral. It irked me that I felt some compassion for the man. He didn't deserve it, but it was mine to give as I chose.

"As the original Angel of Mercy, I give you my blessing, Daisy Leigh Amara Jones." He held up his fading hand to keep me from interrupting. "I'm fully aware how little it means, but I give it nonetheless. At one time, millions of years ago, I deserved the title bestowed upon me. I failed the Universe by handing the precious gift over to Clarissa. For that, I'm ashamed."

My breathing grew labored. His words were far too little, far too late. However, I didn't say a anything to make it easier on him.

"I forced the role upon you. With every fiber of my being, I knew you would fail," he admitted. "You did not. My hateful folly is the Immortal Universe's gain."

He searched my face for a clue as to how I was feeling about his mea culpa. I gave him nothing.

He continued to speak and continued to fade away. "The Angel of Mercy is the role you were destined for. You were created in love by the Archangel Michael and the Death Counselor, Alana Jones. There are no mistakes in the Immortal world. You have and will continue to outshine the damage caused by the ones who came before you. For that I am grateful."

His words might have meant something to me before he'd undermined me and tried to end me. Now... they were just words spoken by a dying man who was desperate to undo some of the ugliness that he'd perpetrated. But like my brother, who had suffered heinously at the hands of Zadkiel far longer than I had, I was a better person than the ghost at my feet.

Squeezing Gideon's hand, I released it and stepped forward. I loved the Grim Reaper. He was one of my reasons for living, along with our daughter, but I was my own woman. I was strong. I was good and I could stand on my own.

"I don't wish you harm," I said. "I don't wish you happiness." I paused and gathered my thoughts. The right thing to do was to rise above the depths of evil that Zadkiel had left in his wake of destruction.

What would feel satisfying in the short term could haunt me for all my years... and I had a lot of those ahead of me. I swallowed and sat down on the floor next to the man who'd been my worst enemy since the day I'd met him. I glanced over at Tory and indicated that she should stop keeping him here. She nodded gratefully and collapsed into Gabe's waiting arms.

Zadkiel's minutes were numbered, but I had more to say. "I wish you nothing," I told him. "It's the most I can give. Forgiveness is complicated. If I said the words you want to hear, it would be a lie. The most I can offer is that I'll accept your apology. I'll work on forgiving you, but there's no guarantee that day will come. If it does, you'll never know."

He whispered something I couldn't make out and watched my every move.

I carried on with the words I needed to say to him before he was gone. "It's an injustice that you won't suffer the consequences for your crimes. The anguish you've caused is embedded deep in those you sinned against.

Although, I suppose the punishment will be that you'll never get the chance at redemption. You lost that chance. You burned it to the ground then stomped in the ashes."

The man gasped and began to cry. A ghost could shed no tears, but his misery was clear.

"Here's what I will do," I said, reaching out and touching what was left of him. He sighed with contentment at my touch. It broke a tiny piece of my heart. "I'll accept the blessing of the man you once were—not the man you've become. I will treasure it and work to be compassionate and kind. I'll defend those I love and live a good life. If I sense I'm falling into the abyss of Immortal madness, I'll leave my position and give it to someone more worthy. I promise I will *never* become the monster that you've become"

"It's more than I asked for and more than I deserve," he replied brokenly.

"True," I agreed. "It's time for you to leave, Zadkiel. May your trip be peaceful."

I kept my hand on him until there was nothing left to touch. The Angel who had hurt so many was now a pile of dust. The man was nonentity. He would not be missed or thought of with kindness or love by a single soul. He'd reaped what he'd sown. The only way a person lived on was in the fond memories of those who loved them. No one loved Zadkiel. It was as tragic as it was fitting. The original Angel of Mercy would never harm anyone again.

Candy Vargo walked around and handed out toothpicks. Everyone took the offering and put them into their mouths. The picture was so absurd, I laughed. I might have started it, but all followed. It was a Mary Tyler Moore/Chuckles the

Clown moment. We laughed until we cried at what amounted to a wake for Zadkiel.

It was cathartic and somehow exactly what was needed.

Candy wiped her tears and burped. It was classic. "I say we blow this fuckin' popsicle stand."

"I couldn't agree more," I announced, holding out my hands. "I don't ever want to see this particular version of my home again."

In a flash of golden glitter—hand in hand, we left the dragon's hoard.

CHAPTER THIRTEEN

THE TRANSPORT HOME HAD BEEN AS BAD AS THE TRIP TO THE parallel plane. Jolly Sue had spoken the words of the spell to leave the hoard, and no one, except the Keeper of Fate, had come through it unscathed. Lura Belle walloped her sister in the head upon arrival back home. She called Jolly Sue a spleeny, unmuzzled horn-beast and insisted that the next time we plane jumped, she would be the one to chant the spell. She claimed she was a better travel guide and wouldn't let her guests feel like they were being burned alive.

There would be no *next time* as far as I was concerned. That chapter was closed... I hoped.

Dimple puked in the kitchen sink. Zander and Catriona went up to our guest rooms to sleep off the horrific journey. Prue, Abby and Rafe followed after our new guests to make sure they were comfortable. Candy Vargo chuckled as she watched Zander try to hold Prue's hand as they departed. It was a developing story that I prayed had a happy ending attached to it. We could all use one of those.

Tory looked exhausted. She'd expended too much magic for the benefit of her worst enemy. I knew she would live with no regrets. She'd said what she wanted to the man who had hurt her beyond comprehension, and she'd given those she cared for the chance to do the same. Gabe hovered over her even though she kept weakly slapping him away.

My brother didn't give up easily. He wore his heart on his sleeve and didn't have any intention of hiding his feelings. They'd been separated for a thousand years due to Zadkiel's psychotic lies. My guess was that if it took a thousand more to win her back, Gabe would gladly do it.

What I wanted now was to live my life in peace for a little while as opposed to pieces. I didn't know who I had to bribe to catch a break, but I was willing to pay the big bucks.

I couldn't believe it was only eight AM in the morning. It felt as if we'd been gone for a year. It had only been a little over twelve hours. None of us had gotten any sleep. I was tired, but wired. Sleep would come soon enough. I needed to bask in the glow of love and friends first. We'd briefed everyone about Zadkiel's end. As expected, no one shed a tear. The Micky Muggles discussion, along with his departing threat to return, would happen after some coffee.

The house was filled with people I loved. Most importantly, Alana Catherine was on her way with our friends who'd protected her while Gideon and I couldn't. My gratitude for them was immense. The safe word had been shared with everyone and we were as secure as we could be at the moment. The thought of holding my baby in my arms again and breastfeeding her made me giddy. Her milk-drunk expression of love was necessary for me to feel whole. Gideon had not let me out of his sight since we'd arrived. He'd opened the front door so many times to check on Alana Catherine's impending arrival, the room was freezing. Charlie just laughed and made a roaring fire in the stone fireplace. The crackle and dancing of the flickering flames were hypnotic.

"Darlings!" Dirk squealed as he strutted into the living room like it was his own personal catwalk. The fabulous queen wore a bright orange sequined ballgown trimmed in marabou. It would have been a hideous eyesore on anyone else. Dirk made it work. "Wonderful news! In celebration of Zadkiel's demise. Tim has prepared a breakfast casserole called Turkey-Noodle-Dooda-Surprise hotdish. Smells divine."

"Debatable," Gideon whispered.

I agreed. "Wait. What does Turkey-Noodle-haha have to do with Zadkiel?"

"It's Turkey-Noodle-Dooda-Surprise hotdish," Dirk corrected me. "And I don't know how it connects to the dead bastard, but our Tim is brilliant and works in mysterious ways. Love him!"

"Is there actually turkey in it?" Heather asked with a small gag as she placed a cool washcloth on Dimple's head and got her comfortable in the overstuffed armchair.

"I have no idea," Dirk admitted with a giggle. "There were so many ingredients I couldn't tell you. But I did notice he used hot sauce and jelly. Simply the best!"

Best wasn't the word I'd use. Inedible was more accurate. Thankfully, turkey-doodle-dodo wasn't in my future. Being a vegetarian rocked.

Heather sat down next to me and leaned close. "I'll go to the Piggly Wiggly in a bit and get something edible."

"Donuts," I whispered. "Glazed."

My sister gave me a thumbs up. "Your wish is my command."

"Turkey-Noodle-Hooha sounds tasty," Candy Vargo said dropping down onto the couch and putting her feet on the coffee table. "I think we need to discuss the fuckin' fucker."

I didn't have the energy to yell at her or knock her feet off the furniture. It also seemed unimportant to clarify that *hooha* was a nick-name for a vagina. The coffee was helping, but there was only so much I could handle on so little sleep.

"Do we have to do it right his minute?" I asked, cuddling up to Gideon on the other couch. "I just want one second to enjoy no one I love being in mortal danger."

I looked up at Gideon's gorgeous face and a smile tugged at the corner of my lips. His eyes were glued to the front door. His anticipation of our daughter coming home made me love the man even more than I already did.

"One question, please," Heather said. "Is Micky Muggles alive or dead?"

"Unclear," Gabe replied. "The gals bit his ass off, so the consensus is that once the rest of the magic fades, he'll revert to true age and die since he has nowhere to store the magic."

"Come again?" Charlie asked, confused. "Did you actually say they *bit* his ass off?"

"Damn straight," Jolly Sue stated with a gag. "Went for the tail like Candy Vargo commanded. It was nasty and the taste wasn't good, but we got the job done."

"Fuckin' gnarly," Candy announced, grinning at the Nephilim. "My gals have big lady-balls and outstandin' chompers."

"The toothpicks were a godsend," Lura Belle commented. "Biting an ass off is more complicated than it sounds. And having ass stuck between your teeth is quite unpleasant."

"In all my centuries I've never heard of anything like this," Charlie muttered, going a little green. "I suppose I was expecting the use of a sword for the removal of the tail... umm... ass."

"A sword would have been a heck of a lot less bloody," Dimple acknowledged. "I still have the taste of metal in my mouth. I'm hopin' the Turkey-Noodle-Dooda-Surprise will take it away."

"Oh shit," I said, getting to my feet. "Did you gals swallow any of his blood? Did you feel any kind of rush?"

Lura Belle wrinkled her brow in thought. "Well, yes. I assumed the rush came from biting an ass off of a person. I've never done that before."

"And I never want to do it again," Dimple choked out, holding her stomach and scurrying to the bathroom.

I was glad she was going to aim for the toilet this time instead of the kitchen sink. Her loud retching made my gag reflex kick in.

"Poor old gal," Dirk said, following her to help out.

"Is the rush an issue?" Gideon asked.

"Possibly," I answered. Lura Belle and Jolly Sue were sprawled out on the love seat. I eyed them warily. "If you swallowed some of his blood, you might have some of his power."

"Oh! Hell's bells," Dimple screeched from the half-bath by the kitchen right before she emptied the contents of her stomach for the third time.

Jolly Sue shook her head and groaned. "I don't want more power. Just got rid of the awful gift I've been stuck with since I was born."

Lura Belle was appalled at the news. "How long will it last?"

"How much do you think you ingested?" I asked.

"Not much," she replied with a shudder of disgust. "I got more on me than in me. Does flesh count as blood because I might have swallowed a section of the butt."

If someone had told me that I'd be talking to a hundred and something year old woman about the finer points of biting off an ass and whether swallowing some of it was a bad thing, I would have punched them in the head. Right now, I would happily punch myself in the head not to have the conversation.

"Candy, can you field that question?" I asked. She'd kind of been there and done that when she'd eaten Gabe, Prue, Abby and Rafe all those years ago.

We were hitting all the gag inducing subjects this morning. I might be joining Dimple in the bathroom shortly.

"Sure," she said, taking the toothpick out of her mouth and tucking it behind her ear. "I'm gonna go with a no on the butt flesh question unless you ate an artery."

"Jesus," Gideon muttered, pressing the bridge of his nose.

"Hey Tim," Candy yelled. "I need some expert advice."

Tim hustled into the living room from the kitchen where he'd been hard at work creating something that smelled really bad. He wore one of my aprons over his mail uniform. "How can I be of service, friend?"

"Does an ass have arteries?" she asked.

Tim thought for a moment, then pulled out the ever-present notebook from one of his many pockets. "Luckily, I've studied the buttock recently. I was searching for a gross fact that might surprise Jennifer and make her laugh." He flipped through the pages. "Ah, here we go. The inferior gluteal artery is in the buttock and supplies oxygenated blood to the glute muscles. So yes, there's an artery."

"Thanks," Candy said.

Tim wasn't done. "And while we're on the subject of butts... a hairy butt actually serves a purpose."

"I'd like to stop you right there," Tory said with a groan.

Tim giggled. "Can you live without knowing why a hirsute bum is a good thing?"

Tory squinted at him and tried not to smile. She failed. It was good to see her happy or, at least, not completely miserable. Gross facts for the win.

"Fine," she conceded. "Tell me about furry rumps. I'm quite sure I'll live to regret asking."

"Very well then," Tim said with a naughty twinkle in his eyes. "The beneficial reason that hair grows on the rear end is severalfold. One, it prevents chafing of the buttock cheeks when you walk or run. As we all know, a chafed butt is a sorry situation. It also has a lovely evolutionary function.

Ass hair holds in your natural scent. This is primal and something that attracts others."

"I'm gonna beg to differ on that," Lura Belle said with a sour expression. "A stinky bum is not attractive."

"I was right," Tory said, shaking her head.

About?" Gabe inquired with a chuckle.

The not-so-icy ice princess smirked, "That I would live to regret asking."

"Live and learn, motherfucker," Candy Vargo said with a laugh. "So, according to Timmy boy, unless y'all swallowed a portion of the ass containing the inferior gluteal artery, you're all good."

Lura Belle opened her mouth to say something else, but changed her mind. She was smarter than she looked.

"How about this?" I suggested, wanting to move on to a new subject. "We'll watch the gals for unusual behavior and deal with it if we have to."

"Agreed," Candy Vargo said. "No use cryin' over spilt milk, bunghole arteries or stank hair up the poop shoot." The Keeper of Fate was always good for a disgusting visual that would stay in your frontal lobe for a while.

The gust of cold wind when the front door flew open made me gasp with joy. Tears filled my eyes. There had been copious tears when Gabe and Prue reunited with Rafe and Abby. The siblings' love ran very deep, but that was nothing compared to the sobs of joy that left my mouth when I saw my baby.

"Special delivery," Jennifer announced with a wide smile as she handed me Alana Catherine. Missy, Amelia, June, Wally, Carl and Fred were right behind her.

Home was finally home. Alana Catherine's sleepy presence made it that way. I was pretty sure Gideon was crying more than me. So much for the Grim Reaper being the stoic bad guy...

"Now the gang is all here," I said with a grin so wide it hurt my cheeks. I held Alana Catherine as Gideon's strong arms wrapped around both of us. I was truly centered and calm for the first time in a while.

"I want to hear everything," June announced as she beelined it for Charlie and gave him a kiss. "I'm just so happy everyone is home and safe."

"Oh yes, sweetikins," Carl squealed as he, Fred and Wally joined Dirk in a drag queen group hug. "We must hear the dish."

"Speaking of," Tim called out from the kitchen. "The Turkey-Noodle-Dooda-Surprise hotdish is almost ready! Hope everyone is hungry. I've made four huge trays!"

"That does not sound good," Missy said before she grabbed Heather and soundly kissed her.

"We're going to the Piggly Wiggly in a sec for a more edible alternative," Heather told her.

Missy laughed. "I'm in."

Amelia glanced around in concern. "Where's Rafe?"

"Upstairs," Candy Vargo told her. "Go on up and kiss your man."

Amelia blushed. "Umm... okay, I think I will." She ran to the base of the stairs then turned back to her new roommate Candy. "Oh, the kids are great. I got everyone off to school this morning."

"Course you did," Candy said with a thumbs up. "You're the baddest of the badasses."

Amelia laughed and raced up the stairs.

"Love that gal like a daughter," Candy said, shaking her head. "Used to think I'd fucked over too many people to deserve anything good, but I got me a whole bunch of kids now. Who woulda thunk it?"

"I woulda thunk it," Gram said as she floated down the stairs with Mr. Jackson. "You might have a potty mouth and crappy manners, but you're as good as gold, Candy Vargo. It just tickles me pink to see you bein' a mamma to Amelia and all them darlin' foster kids. I'm right proud of you, girlie!"

It was the Keeper of Fate's turn to get teary eyed.

June hustled over and put a large container on the coffee table in front of me. Life had just gone from perfect to out of this world.

"Is that what I think it is?" I asked, unable to contain my excitement.

June giggled. "If you think it's a tub of my homemade peanut butter cookies, then yes."

"I already ate a dozen this morning," Jennifer said with a laugh as she pulled a bottle of wine from her purse.

"Dude," I said, squinting at her. "Wine? Really?"

"It's five o'clock somewhere," she replied with a wink. "And I figured we might be having a celebration."

"Hell to the yes, Sugar Pants," Wally announced, snapping his fingers and producing a bottle opener. "I've been beside myself worried. A little vino would be welcome."

Fred and Carl, dressed to the nines in pink velvet mini

dresses and heels ran to the kitchen to get wine glasses for all.

Gideon chuckled and gave me a squeeze. "I suppose getting soused could make the turkey casserole tolerable."

"Not sure anything will make a combo of turkey, jelly, hot sauce and, God only knows what else, tolerable," I told him.

"I think I might have just thrown up in my mouth a little," Tory muttered with a pained laugh.

Heather stood up and grabbed her purse. "And on that note, I'm going to the Piggly Wiggly for donuts. Anybody in?"

"Ohhhh," Fred shrieked, coming back into the living room loaded down with wine glasses. "I'm in, doll face! The Piggly Wiggly is adorable. I picked up some Fruit Loops there last week."

"With what?" I asked with a wince.

Fred was perplexed. "My hands, girlfriend."

"Did you happen to pay for them or did you steal them?" I inquired. The queens weren't used to the social norms of the human world... like paying for things.

"Whoopsie doodle," Fred said with a giggle.

I shook my head and laughed. Alana Catherine cooed. She had no clue what was going on, but joy was contagious... even if it was about pilfering Fruit Loops.

"Did you know that Fruit Loops are all the same flavor?" Jennifer asked as she poured the wine into the glasses.

"Blasphamy!" Wally cried out. "Is this true?"

"One hundred percent," Jennifer assured him. "Also, it's impossible to hum when you're holding your nose."

Of course, everyone in the room tested the theory. She was correct.

"I'm out," Heather said as she opened the front door.

"I'm coming, as well," Missy said.

"Us too!" Dirk exclaimed, hustling his three cohorts out of the door.

"Shall we?" June asked Charlie. "I could use some fresh air."

"We shall," Charlie said with a smile that made his adoration for his wife very clear.

"Well heck," Jennifer said, topping off her wine glass. "If everyone's going, I ain't missin' out on a party!" She scurried out into the cold morning with a glass of wine in true Jennifer fashion.

The crowd had pared down, but it was still a happy home.

Looking down at Alana Catherine, my heart grew bigger. "I love you, baby girl."

Gideon leaned in and kissed her nose. Our gorgeous daughter reached up, grabbed a fistful of his hair and pulled. The Grim Reaper sighed in absolute contentment. Being a daddy was a good look on him.

"Not good. Not good. Not good," Dimple said in a shrill tone, jumping to her feet and walking in circles.

Jolly Sue got down on her hands and knees and began frantically searching for something on the floor. Lura Belle had gone ashen. She grabbed the arms of the love seat and began bouncing her knees spastically.

"What the fuck?" Candy Vargo muttered as she and Gabe rushed to the women.

Gideon immediately took Alana Catherine and covered her with his body. Gram and Mr. Jackson tried their best to calm the old gals, but nothing helped.

"What's happening?" I demanded, trying to get the Nephilim talk to me.

"Don't know. Don't know," Dimple said, joining Jolly Sue on the floor.

"Might be the blood they got in their systems," Gabe said, doing his best to get them off the ground.

Tory, as depleted as she was, approached the panic-stricken old ladies and touched each one of them. Silver crystals formed a small funnel and rained gently down on the trio. Immediately, they grew serene. Gabe grabbed Tory's small frame before she collapsed. Cradling her in his arms he gently placed her on the couch. His features were tight with concern.

Candy Vargo settled the Nephilim back on the loveseat and checked them over. Mr. Jackson and Gram hovered over Tory.

I approached the gals and squatted down to their level. "Do you know what just happened?"

Lura Belle was still pale, but was more herself after Tory had touched her. "I don't. Just got a real bad feeling."

"Real bad," Jolly Sue added.

I glanced over at Candy Vargo.

She shook her head and shrugged. "Don't know." She pulled a handful of toothpicks out and shoved them into her mouth. "Most likely it's a reaction to the blood."

The front door opened, and Heather walked inside. "I'm back."

"That was fast," I said.

She laughed. "Wasn't enough room in the car," she replied, looking around. "What's happening here?"

My phone vibrated in my pocket. I ignored it. I was glad for the extra backup on whatever was going on with the Nephilim. I welcomed my sister's intelligence and intuition. Maybe she could figure out what the hell was happening. "Not exactly sure," I informed her. "They just started acting strange a few seconds ago. Tory tried to help, but her energy is too far drained at this point."

Heather assessed the situation and moved to a very weak and pale Tory. "Get up," she told Gabe. "I want to check her over."

Gabe stood and joined me by the Nephilim. His body was tense and leaving Tory didn't make him happy. However, Heather had powers that could help her. Gabe wouldn't stand in our sister's way.

Tim popped his head into the living room. I was surprised he hadn't heard the ruckus. "Where did everyone go? Food's almost ready."

"Piggly Wiggly," I said, then quickly added. "I think they went to get some dessert." Hurting Tim's feelings wasn't on the table.

My pocket kept buzzing. I briefly wondered if they got to the Piggly Wiggly and had no money. The thought was absurd. While the queens might have sticky fingers, the rest of my crew were law abiding citizens.

"You got a vibratin' dildo in your pants or are you just happy to see me?" Candy inquired with a chuckle.

"Nope," I said with a grin as I pulled out my phone and glanced at it.

I read the text once. Confused, I read it again. Then I read it once more.

My body felt hot. The phone felt like a venomous snake in my hand. My brain raced and my stomach tightened to the point of pain. Breathing was difficult and I pulled from all the power I possessed to stay calm.

"Gideon," I said in an outwardly relaxed tone while my insides screamed in terror. "Alana Catherine needs her diaper changed. Can you take her up and change it, please?"

"Happy to," he said, not noticing my inner-freakout.

That was good. If he didn't notice there was no way anyone else did.

Glancing down at the phone again, I prayed hard that I'd misconstrued what I'd seen. I hadn't. It was a text message from Heather at the Piggly Wiggly asking if I wanted blue-berry donuts as well as glazed. Heather was at the store... but she was also on the couch with Tory, and no one else was in reaching distance except for two ghosts who wouldn't be much help if shit hit the fan.

My fingers began to spark, and my hair blew wildly around my head.

It wasn't Heather sitting on my couch, not unless she could magically be in two places at once. The sick feeling in the pit of my stomach grew until I thought it would swallow me up.

"You okay?" Doppelganger-Heather asked.

I stared at her, trying to keep the rage and fear out of my eyes. "What's the safe word?"

She looked confused.

I didn't back down. My upper lip curled into a snarl. "Tell me the safe word. Now."

Candy Vargo growled deep in her throat. Gabe hissed as his wings burst from his back and his eyes went blindingly gold.

Heather laughed and wrapped her arms around Tory. Her grip was vise-like and Tory tried to move away.

"Tell me the safe word," I ground out.

In less time than it took to inhale, Heather was gone and Micky Muggles was in her place. He was naked and he held a razor-sharp sword to Tory's neck. "Don't make a move or your little buddy is dust," he threatened.

"What do you want?" I snapped.

The blade was too close to Tory's neck to attack and Tory was too weak to fight him off. The sound of fury and agony that came from Gabe chilled me to the bone.

"Immortality," Micky Muggles said. "Isn't that what everyone wants?"

"You ain't got nowhere to store the magic," Candy Vargo hissed. "We removed your tail. You're done, fucker." Sparks popped off of her. "It's only a matter of time." She looked like a deadly crate of fireworks about to explode in every direction and light this place up.

"And that's where you wrong, bitch," Micky Muggles shot back with an oily laugh. He grabbed his dick with his free hand and stroked it. "The tail is in the front."

Lura Belle stepped forward. Dimple and Jolly Sue were at her side. "You take your hands off Tory, you paunchy, ruttish wagtail," she shouted.

"Or what?" he demanded with a raised brow.

"Or you'll regret it with every fiber of your slimy being," I ground out, looking for an opening to blast him without harming Tory.

Gram and Mr. Jackson had attached themselves to Tory to give her comfort. Micky Muggles pressed the sword into Tory's neck. The blade cut into her flesh, and it appeared sharp enough that it wouldn't take much if he wanted to decapitate her.

The shitshow unfolding in front of me was the worst I'd experience. With all the power and magic I had I was helpless. How did a psychotic redneck Nephilim with a mullet keep besting us?

"Here's the deal," Micky said with a wink and a wank. "You figure out how to get Parveit, Lord the Red, true Immortality. I'm gettin' right sick of drinkin' blood all the time."

"And?" I pressed.

"And I won't drain this powerful little Immortal dry," he bargained with a chuckle. The scum leaned over and licked some of the blood gushing from Tory's neck. "Yum. Tasty." He smacked his lips together grossly. "You got one week."

He was stupid. He was an egomaniac. My brain worked overtime to use the knowledge to my advantage. "A week should be enough time," I told him, sounding as casual as I could considering the circumstances. "Where can we find you when we have the spell?"

I was beyond sure that a spell for Immortality didn't exist. However, I was banking on his lack of brain cells and his greed.

"Read the book," he shouted. "It's in the fucking book."

In a blast of dull brown dust, the vile self-proclaimed dragon disappeared with Tory.

Gabe's anguished bellow of fury brought everyone from upstairs racing to the living room. Candy Vargo grabbed Tim, removed him from the kitchen and detonated it. We were lucky the entire house didn't collapse.

"What's going on?" Gideon demanded, holding a crying Alana Catherine in his arms.

"Micky Muggles took Tory," Gabe roared.

"How?" Zander demanded. "He shouldn't have had that much power left."

The Keeper of Fate, still glowing dangerously, answered the question. "The dragon's tail wasn't his ass. It's his dick."

The information caused a moment of appalled silence. My fury and terror for Tory made me itch. I wanted to peel my skin off my body. That would be a bad move. I was going to save that torture for Micky Muggles.

"You've read the book," I said to Candy. "Where would Parveit, Lord of the Red hang out for a week?"

Candy's smile was dastardly. To me it was gorgeous. "Kentucky. Lexington, Kentucky."

"Wait. Where are Gram and Mr. Jackson?" Prue asked.

The need to throw up was real. "Gram?" I called out. "Mr. Jackson? I need you to show yourselves. Now. Please."

Nothing.

Gabe punched a hole in the plaster then walked to the center of the gathered group. "I'm leaving. I want the Nephilim and Candy Vargo with me. The Nephilim can feel the bastard's presence. I'm sure that's why they freaked out."

Gabe's wings vibrated with power and his golden eyes narrowed to slits. "I will find him and I will end him."

The front door opened and the crew from the Piggly Wiggly entered. Their gazes immediately fell upon the golden-glowing Archangel. He was lit up like a Christmas tree, and he had the floor.

"What did we miss?" Heather asked, feeling the dark mood.

"Micky Muggles took Tory and possibly Gram and Mr. Jackson," I filled them in.

"Where?" Charlie demanded.

"Lexington, Kentucky," Candy answered.

I looked into the Immortal Enforcer's eyes. "Tell me the safe word."

"Toothpick," Charlie replied without hesitation.

Taking Alana Catherine from Gideon's arms, I handed her to Charlie. "Take her back to Candy's. Drop a ward around the house and protect her with your life."

"As you wish," Charlie said, disappearing in a haze of silver mist.

"The rest of you stay here. If Gram or Mr. Jackson show up, call me," I ordered.

"We're going to Kentucky?" Gideon asked.

"Yep," I said, taking his hand in mine then reaching for Gabe's. "It's time to slay the dragon for good."

This time there would be no mercy.

The End... for now.
You want to know what happens next? Go HERE for the next book in the series!

NEXT IN THE GOOD TO THE LAST DEATH SERIES

ROBYN'S BOOK LIST

(IN CORRECT READING ORDER)

HOT DAMNED SERIES
Fashionably Dead
Fashionably Dead Down Under
Hell on Heels
Fashionably Dead in Diapers
A Fashionably Dead Christmas
Fashionably Hotter Than Hell
Fashionably Dead and Wed
Fashionably Fanged
Fashionably Flawed
A Fashionably Dead Diary
Fashionably Forever After
Fashionably Fabulous
A Fashionable Fiasco
Fashionably Fooled
Fashionably Dead and Loving It
Fashionably Dead and Demonic

The Oh My Gawd Couple
A Fashionable Disaster
Fashionably Fierce

GOOD TO THE LAST DEMON SERIES
As the Underworld Turns
The Edge of Evil
The Bold and the Banished
Guiding Blight

GOOD TO THE LAST DEATH SERIES
It's a Wonderful Midlife Crisis
Whose Midlife Crisis Is It Anyway?
A Most Excellent Midlife Crisis
My Midlife Crisis, My Rules
You Light Up My Midlife Crisis
It's A Matter of Midlife and Death
The Facts Of Midlife
It's A Hard Knock Midlife
Run for Your Midlife
It's A Hell of A Midlife
A Leaner Meaner Midlife

MY SO-CALLED MYSTICAL MIDLIFE SERIES
The Write Hook
You May Be Write
All The Write Moves
My Big Fat Hairy Wedding
Johnson Jones's Diary

SHIFT HAPPENS SERIES
Ready to Were
Some Were in Time
No Were To Run
Were Me Out
Were We Belong

MAGIC AND MAYHEM SERIES
Switching Hour
Witch Glitch
A Witch in Time
Magically Delicious
A Tale of Two Witches
Three's A Charm
Switching Witches
You're Broom or Mine?
The Bad Boys of Assjacket
The Newly Witch Game
Witches In Stitches

SEA SHENANIGANS SERIES
Tallulah's Temptation
Ariel's Antics
Misty's Mayhem
Petunia's Pandemonium
Jingle Me Balls

A WYLDE PARANORMAL SERIES
Beauty Loves the Beast

HANDCUFFS AND HAPPILY EVER AFTERS SERIES
How Hard Can it Be?
Size Matters
Cop a Feel

If after reading all the above you are still wanting more adventure and zany fun, read *Pirate Dave and His Randy Adventures*, the romance novel budding novelist Rena helped wicked Evangeline write in *How Hard Can It Be?*

Warning: Pirate Dave Contains Romance Satire, Spoofing, and Pirates with Two Pork Swords.

EXCERPT: THE WRITE HOOK

BOOK DESCRIPTION

THE WRITE HOOK

Midlife is full of surprises. Not all of them are working for me.

At forty-two I've had my share of ups and downs. Relatively normal, except when the definition of normal changes... drastically.

NYT Bestselling Romance Author: Check
Amazing besties: Check
Lovely home: Check
Pet cat named Thick Stella who wants to kill me: Check
Wacky Tabacky Dealing Aunt: Check
Cheating husband banging the weather girl on our kitchen table: Check
Nasty Divorce: Oh yes
Characters from my novels coming to life: Umm... yes
Crazy: Possibly

Four months of wallowing in embarrassed depression should be enough. I'm beginning to realize that no one is who they seem to be, and my life story might be spinning out of my control. It's time to take a shower, put on a bra, and wear something other than sweatpants. Difficult, but doable.

With my friends—real and imaginary—by my side, I need to edit my life before the elusive darkness comes for all of us.

The plot is no longer fiction. It's my reality, and I'm writing a happy ever after no matter what. I just have to find the *write hook*.

CHAPTER 1

"I didn't leave that bowl in the sink," I muttered to no one as I stared in confusion at the blue piece of pottery with milk residue in the bottom. "Wait. Did I?"

Slowly backing away, I ran my hands through my hair that hadn't seen a brush in days—possibly longer—and decided that I wasn't going to think too hard about it. Thinking led to introspective thought, which led to dealing with reality, and that was a no-no.

Reality wasn't my thing right now.

Maybe I'd walked in my sleep, eaten a bowl of cereal, then politely put the bowl in the sink. It was possible.

"That has to be it," I announced, walking out of the kitchen and avoiding all mirrors and any glass where I could catch a glimpse of myself.

It was time to get to work. Sadly, books didn't write themselves.

"I can do this. I have to do this." I sat down at my desk

and made sure my posture didn't suck. I was fully aware it would suck in approximately five minutes, but I wanted to start out right. It would be a bad week to throw my back out. "Today, I'll write ten thousand words. They will be coherent. I will not mistakenly or on purpose make a list of the plethora of ways I would like to kill Darren. He's my past. Beheading him is illegal. I'm far better than that. On a more positive note, my imaginary muse will show his pony-tailed, obnoxious ass up today, and I won't play Candy Jelly Crush until the words are on the page."

Two hours later...

Zero words. However, I'd done three loads of laundry—sweatpants, t-shirts and underwear—and played Candy Jelly Crush until I didn't have any more lives. As pathetic as I'd become, I hadn't sunk so low as to purchase new lives. That would mean I'd hit rock bottom. Of course, I was precariously close, evidenced by my cussing out of the Jelly Queen for ten minutes, but I didn't pay for lives. I considered it a win.

I'd planned on folding the laundry but decided to vacuum instead. I'd fold the loads by Friday. It was Tuesday. That was reasonable. If they were too wrinkled, I'd simply wash them again. No biggie. After the vacuuming was done, I rearranged my office for thirty minutes. I wasn't sure how to Feng Shui, but after looking it up on my phone, I gave it a half-assed effort.

Glancing around at my handiwork, I nodded. "Much better. If the surroundings are aligned correctly, the words will flow magically. I hope."

Two hours later...

"Mother humper," I grunted as I pushed my monstrosity of a bed from one side of the bedroom to the other. "This weighs a damn ton."

I'd burned all the bedding seven weeks ago. The bonfire had been cathartic. I'd taken pictures as the five hundred thread count sheets had gone up in flame. I'd kept the comforter. I'd paid a fortune for it. It had been thoroughly saged and washed five times. Even though there was no trace of Darren left in the bedroom, I'd been sleeping in my office.

The house was huge, beautiful... and mine—a gorgeously restored Victorian where I'd spent tons of time as a child. It had an enchanted feel to it that I adored. I didn't need such an enormous abode, but I loved the location—the middle of nowhere. The internet was iffy, but I solved that by going into town to the local coffee shop if I had something important to download or send.

Darren, with the wandering pecker, thought he would get a piece of the house. He was wrong. I'd inherited it from my whackadoo grandmother and great-aunt Flip. My parents hadn't always been too keen on me spending so much time with Granny and Aunt Flip growing up, but I adored the two old gals so much they'd relented. Since I spent a lot of time in an imaginary dream world, my mom and dad were delighted when I related to actual people— even if they were left of center.

Granny and Flip made sure the house was in my name only—nontransferable and non-sellable. It was stipulated that I had to pass it to a family member or the Historical Society when I died. Basically, I had life rights. It was as if

Granny and Aunt Flip had known I would waste two decades of my life married to a jackhole who couldn't keep his salami in his pants and would need someplace to live. God rest Granny's insane soul. Aunt Flip was still kicking, although I hadn't seen her in a few years.

Aunt Flip put the K in kooky. She'd bought a cottage in the hills about an hour away and grew medicinal marijuana—before it was legal. The old gal was the black sheep of the family and preferred her solitude and her pot to company. She hadn't liked Darren a bit. She and Granny both had worn black to my wedding. Everyone had been appalled—even me—but in the end, it made perfect sense. I had to hand it to the old broads. They'd been smarter than me by a long shot. And the house? It had always been my charmed haven in the storm.

Even though there were four spare bedrooms plus the master suite, I chose my office. It felt safe to me.

Thick Stella preferred my office, and I needed to be around something that had a heartbeat. It didn't matter that Thick Stella was bitchy and swiped at me with her deadly kitty claws every time I passed her. I loved her. The feeling didn't seem mutual, but she hadn't left me for a twenty-three-year-old with silicone breast implants and huge, bright white teeth.

"Thick Stella, do you think Sasha should wear red to her stepmother's funeral?" I asked as I plopped down on my newly Feng Shuied couch and narrowly missed getting gouged by my cat. "Yes or no? Hiss at me if it's a yes. Growl at me if it's a no."

Thick Stella had a go at her privates. She was useless.

"That wasn't an answer." I grabbed my laptop from my desk. Deciding it was too dangerous to sit near my cat, I settled for the love seat. The irony of the piece of furniture I'd chosen didn't escape me.

"I think she should wear red," I told Thick Stella, who didn't give a crap what Sasha wore. "Her stepmother was an asshat, and it would show fabu disrespect."

Typing felt good. Getting lost in a story felt great. I dressed Sasha in a red Prada sheath, then had her behead her ex-husband with a dull butter knife when he and his bimbo showed up unexpectedly to pay their respects at the funeral home. It was a bloodbath. Putting Sasha in red was an excellent move. The blood matched her frock to a T.

Quickly rethinking the necessary murder, I moved the scene of the decapitation to the empty lobby of the funeral home. It would suck if I had to send Sasha to prison. She hadn't banged Damien yet, and everyone was eagerly awaiting the sexy buildup—including me. It was the fourth book in the series, and it was about time they got together. The sexual tension was palpable.

"What in the freaking hell?" I snapped my laptop shut and groaned. "Sasha doesn't have an ex-husband. I can't do this. I've got nothing." Where was my muse hiding? I needed the elusive imaginary idiot if I was going to get any writing done. "Chauncey, dammit, where are you?"

"My God, you're loud, Clementine," a busty, beautiful woman dressed in a deep purple Regency gown said with an eye roll.

She was seated on the couch next to Thick Stella, who barely acknowledged her. My cat attacked strangers and friends. Not today. My fat feline simply glanced over at the intruder and yawned. The cat was a traitor.

Forget the furry betrayer. How in the heck did the woman get into my house—not to mention my office—without me seeing her enter? For a brief moment, I wondered if she'd banged my husband too but pushed the sordid thought out of my head. She looked to be close to thirty—too old for the asshole.

"Who are you?" I demanded, holding my laptop over my head as a weapon.

If I threw it and it shattered, I would be screwed. I couldn't remember the last time I'd backed it up. If I lost the measly, somewhat disjointed fifty thousand words I'd written so far, I'd have to start over. That wouldn't fly with my agent or my publisher.

"Don't be daft," the woman replied. "It's rather unbecoming. May I ask a question?"

"No, you may not," I shot back, trying to place her.

She was clearly a nutjob. The woman was rolling up on thirty but had the vernacular of a seventy-year-old British society matron. She was dressed like she'd walked off the set of a film starring Emma Thompson. Her blonde hair shone to the point of absurdity and was twisted into an elaborate up-do. Wispy tendrils framed her perfectly heart-shaped face. Her sparkling eyes were lavender, enhanced by the over-the-top gown she wore.

Strangely, she was vaguely familiar. I just couldn't remember how I knew her.

"How long has it been since you attended to your hygiene?" she inquired.

Putting my laptop down and picking up a lamp, I eyed her. I didn't care much for the lamp or her question. I had been thinking about Marie Condo-ing my life, and the lamp didn't bring me all that much joy. If it met its demise by use of self-defense, so be it. "I don't see how that's any of your business, lady. What I'd suggest is that you leave. Now. Or else I'll call the police. Breaking and entering is a crime."

She laughed. It sounded like freaking bells. Even though she was either a criminal or certifiable, she was incredibly charming.

"Oh dear," she said, placing her hand delicately on her still heaving, milky-white bosom. "You are so silly. The constable knows quite well that I'm here. He advised me to come."

"The constable?" I asked, wondering how far off her rocker she was.

She nodded coyly. "Most certainly. We're all terribly concerned."

I squinted at her. "About my hygiene?"

"That, amongst other things," she confirmed. "Darling girl, you are not an ace of spades or, heaven forbid, an adventuress. Unless you want to be an ape leader, I'd recommend bathing."

"Are you right in the head?" I asked, wondering where I'd left my damn cell phone. It was probably in the laundry room. I was going to be murdered by a nutjob, and I'd lost my chance to save myself because I'd been playing Candy Jelly Crush. The headline would be horrifying—*Homeless-looking, Hygiene-free Paranormal Romance Author Beheaded by Victorian Psycho.*

If I lived through the next hour, I was deleting the game for good.

"I think it would do wonders for your spirit if you donned a nice tight corset and a clean chemise," she suggested, skillfully ignoring my question. "You must pull yourself together. Your behavior is dicked in the nob."

I sat down and studied her. My about-to-be-murdered radar relaxed a tiny bit, but I kept the lamp clutched tightly in my hand. My gut told me she wasn't going to strangle me. Of course, I could be mistaken, but Purple Gal didn't seem violent—just bizarre. Plus, the lamp was heavy. I could knock her ladylike ass out with one good swing.

How in the heck did I know her? College? Grad School? The grocery store? At forty-two, I'd met a lot of people in my life. Was she with the local community theater troop? I was eighty-six percent sure she wasn't here to off me. However, I'd been wrong about life-altering events before— like not knowing my husband was boffing someone young enough to have been our daughter.

"What language are you speaking?" I spotted a pair of scissors on my desk. If I needed them, it was a quick move to grab them. I'd never actually killed anyone except in fictitious situations, but there was a first time for everything.

Pulling an embroidered lavender hankey from her cleavage, she clutched it and twisted it in her slim fingers. "Clementine, *you* should know."

"I'm at a little disadvantage here," I said, fascinated by the batshit crazy woman who'd broken into my home. "You seem to know my name, but I don't know yours."

And that was when the tears started. Hers. Not mine.

"Such claptrap. How very unkind of you, Clementine," she burst out through her stupidly attractive sobs.

It was ridiculous how good the woman looked while crying. I got all blotchy and red, but not the mystery gal in purple. She grew even more lovely. It wasn't fair. I still had no clue what the hell she was talking about, but on the off chance she might throw a tantrum if I asked more questions, I kept my mouth shut.

And yes, she had a point, but my *hygiene* was none of her damn business. I couldn't quite put my finger on the last time I'd showered. If I had to guess, it was probably in the last five to twelve days. I was on a deadline for a book. To be more precise, I was late for my deadline on a book. I didn't exactly have time for personal sanitation right now.

And speaking of deadlines…

"How about this?" My tone was excessively polite. I almost laughed. The woman had illegally entered my house, and I was behaving like she was a guest. "I'll take a shower later today after I get through a few pivotal chapters. Right now, you should leave so I can work."

"Yes, of course," she replied, absently stroking Fat Stella, who purred. If I'd done that, I would be minus a finger. "It would be dreadfully sad if you were under the hatches."

I nodded. "Right. That would, umm… suck."

The woman in purple smiled. It was radiant, and I would have sworn I heard birds happily chirping. I was losing it.

"Excellent," she said, pulling a small periwinkle velvet bag from her cleavage. I wondered what else she had stored in there and hoped there wasn't a weapon. "I shall leave you with two gold coins. While the Grape Nuts were tasty, I would prefer that you purchase some Lucky Charms. I understand they are magically delicious."

"It was you?" I asked, wildly relieved that I hadn't been sleep eating. I had enough problems at the moment. Gaining weight from midnight dates with cereal wasn't on the to-do list.

"It was," she confirmed, getting to her feet and dropping the coins into my hand. "The consistency was quite different from porridge, but I found it tasty—very crunchy."

"Right... well... thank you for putting the bowl in the sink." Wait. Why the hell was I thanking her? She'd wandered in and eaten my Grape Nuts.

"You are most welcome, Clementine," she said with a disarming smile that lit up her unusual eyes. "It was lovely finally meeting you even if your disheveled outward show is entirely astonishing."

I was reasonably sure I had just been insulted by the cereal lover, but it was presented with excellent manners. However, she did answer a question. We hadn't met. I wasn't sure why she seemed familiar. The fact that she knew my name was alarming.

"Are you a stalker?" I asked before I could stop myself.

I'd had a few over the years. Being a *New York Times* bestselling author was something I was proud of, but it had come with a little baggage here and there. Some people seemed to have difficulty discerning fiction from reality. If I had to guess, I'd say Purple Gal might be one of those people.

I'd only written one Regency novel, and that had been at the beginning of my career, before I'd found my groove in paranormal romance. I was way more comfortable writing about demons and vampires than people dressed in top hats and hoopskirts. Maybe the crazy woman had read my first book. It hadn't done well, and for good reason. It was over-the-top bad. I'd blocked the entire novel out of my mind. Live and learn. It had been my homage to Elizabeth Hoyt well over a decade ago. It had been clear to all that I should leave Regency romance to the masters.

"Don't be a Merry Andrew," the woman chided me. "Your bone box is addled. We must see to it at once. I shall pay a visit again soon."

The only part of her gibberish I understood was that she thought she was coming back. Note to self—change all the locks on the doors. Since it wasn't clear if she was packing heat in her cleavage, I just smiled and nodded.

"Alrighty then…" I was unsure if I should walk her to the door or if she would let herself out. Deciding it would be better to make sure she actually left instead of letting her hide in my pantry to finish off my cereal, I gestured to the door. "Follow me."

Thick Stella growled at me. I was so tempted to flip her off but thought it might earn another lecture from Purple Gal. It was more than enough to be lambasted for my appearance. I didn't need my manners picked apart by someone with a tenuous grip on reality.

My own grip was dubious as it was.

"You might want to reconsider breaking into homes," I said, holding the front door open. "It could end badly—for you."

Part of me couldn't believe that I was trying to help the

nutty woman out, but I couldn't seem to stop myself. I kind of liked her.

"I'll keep that in mind," she replied as she sauntered out of my house into the warm spring afternoon. "Remember, Clementine, there is always sunshine after the rain."

As she made her way down the long sunlit, tree-lined drive, she didn't look back. It was disturbingly like watching the end of a period movie where the heroine left her old life behind and walked proudly toward her new and promising future.

Glancing around for a car, I didn't spot one. Had she left it parked on the road so she could make a clean getaway after she'd bludgeoned me? Had I just politely escorted a murderer out of my house?

Had I lost it for real?

Probably.

As she disappeared from sight, I felt the weight of the gold coins still clutched in my hand. Today couldn't get any stranger.

At least, I hoped not.

Opening my fist to examine the coins, I gasped. "What in the heck?"

There was nothing in my hand.

Had I dropped them? Getting down on all fours, I searched. Thick Stella joined me, kind of—more like watched me as I crawled around and wondered if anything that had just happened had actually happened.

"Purple Gal gave me coins to buy Lucky Charms," I told my cat, my search now growing frantic. "You saw her do it. Right? She sat next to you. And you didn't attack her. *Right?*"

Thick Stella simply stared at me. What did I expect? If my cat answered me, I'd have to commit myself. That option might still be on the table. Had I just imagined the entire exchange with the strange woman? Should I call the cops?

"And tell them what?" I asked, standing back up and locking the front door securely. "That a woman in a purple gown broke in and ate my cereal while politely insulting my hygiene? Oh, and she left me two gold coins that disappeared in my hand as soon as she was out of sight? That's not going to work."

I'd call the police if she came back, since I wasn't sure she'd been here at all. She hadn't threatened to harm me. Purple Gal had been charming and well-mannered the entire time she'd badmouthed my cleanliness habits. And to be quite honest, real or not, she'd made a solid point. I could use a shower.

Maybe four months of wallowing in self-pity and only living inside the fictional worlds I created on paper had taken more of a toll than I was aware of. Getting lost in my stories was one of my favorite things to do. It had saved me more than once over the years. It was possible that I'd let it go too far. Hence, the Purple Gal hallucination.

Shit.

First things first. Delete Candy Jelly Crush. Getting rid of the white noise in my life was the first step to... well, the first step to something.

I'd figure it out later.

HIT HERE TO ORDER THE WRITE HOOK!!!!!

NOTE FROM THE AUTHOR

If you enjoyed reading *It's A Hell of a Midlife*, please consider leaving a positive review or rating on the site where you purchased it. Reader reviews help my books continue to be valued by resellers and help new readers make decisions about reading them.

You are the reason I write these stories and I sincerely appreciate each of you!

Many thanks for your support,
~ Robyn Peterman

Want to hear about my new releases?
Visit https://robynpeterman.com/newsletter/ and join my mailing list!

ABOUT ROBYN PETERMAN

Robyn Peterman writes because the people inside her head won't leave her alone until she gives them life on paper. Her addictions include laughing really hard with friends, shoes (the expensive kind), Target, Coke (the drink not the drug LOL) with extra ice in a Yeti cup, bejeweled reading glasses, her kids, her super-hot hubby and collecting stray animals.

A former professional actress with Broadway, film and T.V. credits, she now lives in the South with her family and too many animals to count.

Writing gives her peace and makes her whole, plus having a job where she can work in sweatpants works really well for her.

Made in United States
Orlando, FL
17 October 2023